FOR YOUR EARS ONLY

IVORY TOWER SPIES BOOK ONE

EMILY KAZMIERSKI

For E and S, may you grow and move in the world in a way that leaves everyone you meet a little brighter for having spent time with you.

Chapter 1

In November of 1971 a man named Dan Cooper hijacked an airplane and was never found. I'm about to do the same thing.

I look toward the front of the Cessna Grand Caravan I'm sitting in, at the pilot and four other passengers. The man directly in front of me, Mr. Wong, is wearing a charcoal suit with an electric blue shirt and tie. Even though I can't see it at the moment, the color of the shirt is burned into my eyeballs. The young woman in the seat across from him is his secretary, a wrap dress and kitten heels her outfit of choice. The two men sitting near the front of the cabin wear bland black suits with white shirts and black ties. They're Mr. Wong's bodyguards. They won't like me very much in about twenty minutes, after the tranquilizer wears off.

The flight from Ronald Reagan to JFK is a quick one, so I have to make my move. I unbuckle my seatbelt without making a sound and take my backpack from under my seat. Strapping it on over my black pantsuit without drawing attention is tricky, but I manage. My helmet is snug over my wavy blonde wig and my goggles slide into place over my eyes. Last, I unzip the storage pouch on my backpack and take out my tranquilizer gun. If Mr. Wong's bodyguards are worth the money he pays them, they'll know it's not a real gun in less than a second, so I won't give them the chance. I stand quickly, holding my gun up.

Whizz.

Whizz.

Whizz.

Whizz.

Mr. Wong, his assistant, and his two hulking bodyguards slump in their seats, the tranquilizers taking instant effect.

The pilot doesn't turn around. The buzz of the aircraft has muffled the sound of my shots. I've got ten minutes.

I step carefully toward Mr. Wong, whose mouth is hanging open. Kneeling at his feet, I pick the lock on the handcuffs connecting his hands to the briefcase he's holding, and click them into place around my own wrist.

I take a step back from him so that all five people on board are in my peripheral vision. Now all I've got to do is get the pilot's attention. "Don't panic, Mr. Booth," I yell over the whirr of the small plane.

"What?" The pilot glances over his shoulder, then does a double take. His eyes widen as he sees four of his passengers unconscious in their tan leather seats, a tranquilizer dart sticking out of each of them. His eyes lock on me.

"Don't panic." My voice is steady, reassuring.

He gulps once, then turns to face the front.

In slow, calculated movements, I work my way toward the front of the plane. "Descend to 15,000 feet."

"What?" The pilot calls over his shoulder.

"Descend to 15,000 feet."

"No." He yells back, shaking his head. He's not Mr. Wong's usual pilot; he's a stand-in. Mr. Wong's preferred pilot is out with food poisoning. Contaminated chicken salad, so I've been told. A smirk plays on my lips.

I'm guessing, unlike the mounds of men in the seats at Mr. Booth's back, this guy won't know the difference between a tranq gun and a water gun. And the slight trembling in his arms gives him away. Despite his show of obstinacy, he's terrified. It's a condition I can use to get this job done.

"Do it, or you'll regret it." I aim the tranquilizer gun directly at him.

The guy's neck and shoulders tense under his headphones. He's thinking about my threat.

I wait a beat, watching him, enveloped in the loud buzzing of the plane.

The pilot grips the steering wheel tightly. He's going to make a move.

I tighten my hands around my gun, taking aim at his back. My armpits start to sweat under the layers of clothing. I can't really shoot the pilot, so my threat had better land. "Don't do that. You and everyone else on this plane will die."

His shoulders sag, but his hands remain tight around the plane's yoke. "All right," he says after a moment. "I'm descending now. It will take five minutes."

I glance out the window to the darkened sky. The lights of New York are rising to greet us. He's doing as he said he would, but not fast enough.

"Hurry." My grip on my gun is steady, confident. I can do this.

"15,000 feet," the pilot yells back to me.

"Depressurize the cabin."

"What?" His voice is cracked, strangled by fear.

"Do it."

The pilot mumbles something to himself that I can't hear. "Depressurizing now."

I step backward without taking my eyes off the five people in front of me. I can't risk one of them waking up early. Tranquilizing is not an exact science; it depends on the person's weight and metabolism, and Wong's bodyguards are pretty hefty dudes.

"It's done." The pilot risks a glance back at me. "Now what?"

I position myself next to the back door of the plane, grip the handle, and pull. A gust of wind thrusts me back into the cabin. The humidity in the plane spikes, sticking the fine strands of my wig to the back of my neck. Gripping the briefcase with one hand, I holster my tranquilizer gun with the other. Then I rest my free hand on the ceiling of the plane. With one more glance at the passengers in the cabin I'm about to vacate, I throw myself out the plane's door and hurtle toward the earth. I've done it, without a hitch. Grandpa would be proud.

The ground beneath me is a dark, unlit mass. It jumps up to greet me. In my head I'm counting down. I have about thirty seconds of freefall before I need to deploy my parachute. I curl my legs up toward my butt and lift my arms parallel to my head.

I deploy my parachute and the jolt in my pelvis is painful, but welcome. The round, dark green of the canopy balloons above me as it fills with air, slowing my fall to the ground.

I steer the chute with one hand and bring my other wrist to my face. "I'm descending now." I say into my smart watch.

"It's about time," Lotus's voice is hard to hear, but I make it out. I take a deep breath. This mission is almost over.

There's more to Dan Cooper's story than the FBI ever figured out. First off, that wasn't his real name, and he wasn't a hijacker. He was a retired CIA operative who had taken a job for a client. His role was to steal something from a passenger on the plane. The ransom and escape in midair were just theatrics. My grandpa was a dramatic person.

Wharton State Forest looms beneath me, its pine trees spindly in the cold night air. I steer toward the walking trail and brace myself as I near the ground, bending my knees slightly. Even so, once my feet hit the hard-packed dirt path, my legs buckle. I've done this a hundred times and still can't stick the landing.

Moving with precision, I roll up the parachute and stuff it into the backpack. I don't have time to double check my work now; I'll have to do it later.

I push a button on my watch to send my location to Lotus, who is waiting for me at the outskirts of the forest, and say, "Be there in seven minutes."

I scan the forest around me and see no one. It's pitch dark between the trees at this time of night, but then I see the blink-and-you'll-miss-them twinkles of fireflies in the darkest spaces, and a smile spreads across my face. I've always loved those little things, ever since I was a small child. My dad used to take my sister and me out to watch the fireflies before bedtime, and we'd spin among the trees trying to count the glimmering bugs.

Police sirens in the not-so-far distance cut through the calm, reminding me that I'm working and have to focus. There's only one reason the police would be heading toward the forest tonight, and that's the acrobatic escape I just made. The sirens are much closer than I would like. A look at my watch shows me Lotus's location, and I sprint toward it. It's going to be a close one. I pump my legs over the flat ground, the pine needles crunching under my feet.

The sirens are getting closer. They must be driving around the perimeter of the forest. Luckily they have no idea where I am within the mass of trees.

I'm almost to Lotus's location.

I breathe easily as I reach the clearing in the trees. I've always been a great runner.

And there it is: the black sedan is parked at the side of the road, waiting.

Clarity swings open the car's back passenger door and I jump inside. "Go," I say.

She pulls a handcuff key out of my utility belt, which she's got across her lap, and unlocks the handcuff from my hand. Bending down, she slides the slim briefcase under the driver's seat, out of sight.

Lotus maneuvers the car down the road, driving calmly at the speed limit. Any too-fast movement on his part would attract attention from the police.

"Take these off," Clarity says as she deftly unfastens my helmet and taps my goggles. The cuff of her feather-soft, cable-knit sweater grazes my cheek as she works. I pull them over my head, followed by my parachute backpack. Even in a hurry, she finds little ways to take care of me. "It's what sisters are for," she often says.

I reach up to remove the wig, but she stops me. "I'll do it." Carefully but quickly, she takes off the wig I'm wearing and sets it into the round wig box on the seat beside her. Clarity's wigs are her most prized possessions, which is good, because if they weren't they'd end up on the floor of our room like all her other stuff.

I run my fingers through my bleached blonde faux hawk, fluffing up my hair. It's pretty flat after being in a wig all day, and my entire scalp tingles.

"Your suit too," Clarity says.

I shrug off the suit jacket and unbutton my blouse. I don't

even have to check the mirror to make sure Lotus isn't sneaking a peek. He's like my brother.

I pull on the band T-shirt Clarity is holding out to me. My eyes go to hers. "Is this Vale's?"

She shrugs. "It makes you look like a normal teenager."

I nod. It's true. My normal black on black on black with a gray trench doesn't scream well-adjusted adolescent. I make sure the shirt is in place. "It's safe," I say, glancing toward Lotus. "You can use your rearview mirror now."

He grins at me. "Did you get it?"

"Of course." I point down to where the briefcase is hidden.

"Nice." Lotus bobs his head.

Clarity pats me on the leg and gives me a smile. "Dad will be proud of you, Loveday."

A proud smile comes to my face. "Yeah." I relax against the back of the seat and buckle myself in. I've never stolen something from a passenger mid-flight and parachuted to safety before today, but I have to say, it was awesome. And our client will be happy to hear that we've retrieved the stolen design plans and are returning them.

"Our client is going to be so pumped," Lotus says as he drums the steering wheel, but his enthusiasm wanes as we turn a corner and red and blue beams fill our car. A row of police vehicles blocks our way.

"Keep cool," he says without looking back at us. He creeps forward at five miles per hour until an officer lifts a stop sign.

Lotus eases on the brakes and rolls down the window, being careful to keep his hands on the steering wheel. "Good evening, officer."

The officer bends over to peer into the car, first at Lotus

and then at Clarity and me. "What are you kids doing out here after dark?"

"Stargazing for our Earth science class," Lotus says, his tone even. To back up his claim, he holds up an Earth science textbook that had been sitting on the front passenger seat. "What's going on?"

"Just a routine check-point." The officer looks at Clarity and me again, more carefully. Then his gaze moves back to Lotus. "Be careful. You never know what you might find out here at night."

"Yes, sir." Lotus nods. "Thanks."

"Move along, then." The officer waves his arm for us to proceed past the line of squad cars, their blue and red lights painting our faces garish shades.

I take a deep breath once we're clear. That was close.

The FBI won't be thrilled when they can't find a trace of the hijacker's whereabouts. Royal, my dad, is back at the Ivory Tower, probably burning my identity right now.

Speaking of. I tap my watch to send a message the Ivory Tower, home base.

Me
I picked up some asparagus.

We don't use cringeworthy phrases like, "The eagle has landed." No real spies do that. It's way too cheesy. Instead, we say things like, "I forgot to walk the dog," when something goes sideways, or "I got an A in chemistry," when a mission is going well. Royal says it's all about plausible deniability. But honestly, I think he just likes annoying his contact at the CIA by including nonsensical stuff in his reports.

My watch buzzes.

Control
Awesome. I love asparagus.

I smile. That's not Royal responding. It's too enthusiastic for that. Instead, my boyfriend Vale is minding the comms tonight. Beautiful, heart-stopping Vale. I push the image of him out of my mind, slow my heart rate, and relax the muscles in my face. Royal would kill me if he knew Vale and I were... But he won't find out. Not even Clarity knows. I peek at her out of my peripheral vision, but she's busy finessing the wig's position in its box.

I open the news feed on my watch and read the top headlines. Sure enough, the plane hijacking is the biggest news of the night, and local law enforcement is already working with the FBI to coordinate a search of Wharton State Forest. Too bad they'll never find me.

Chapter 2

I lean back against the headrest and close my eyes.

Beside me, the rustling of pages alerts me to the fact that Clarity has pulled out a book. Knowing her, it's probably by a woman who should be more famous than she is. I open my eyes a slit and glance toward her.

Sure enough, she's reading Zora Neale Hurston's *Their Eyes Were Watching God*, which I've read. "Have you noticed that she associates each of her lovers with certain foods?" I ask.

Clarity glances over at me. "Really?"

I nod. "Yeah, consider her nicknames for each guy, especially Tea Cake, and how it correlates to her relationships with them."

"Hmm." Clarity turns back to her book and I shut my eyes. I should have brought one of the worn, clothbound books that I got from my mom, one of the few remaining signs that she existed. One book—Elizabeth Goudge's *The Little White Horse*—is where I got my name. Loveday for Loveday Minette. It's not my real name. Only Royal and Clarity know the name on my birth certificate, and I've decided never to tell anyone else what it is. My mother gave it to me, and it's mine to keep.

My eyes grow heavy as the adrenaline coursing through me abates, and I stare through the window at the shroud of darkness outside. It'll take us almost three hours to get from Wharton Forest back to Georgetown, so I might as well catch a few Zs.

At the sensation of the car pulling to a stop, my eyes open. Lotus has parallel parked out front of a drug store. It's 23:00 and the streets are still dotted with cars trying to get home from work, trying to get to the hotel, or simply cruising. The city never sleeps. At least, not if you know where to look.

"Why are we stopping?" I ask, sitting forward in my seat to peer through the car's windshield.

Clarity pulls me back into my seat with a gentle hand. "I asked him to stop. There are a couple of products I'd like to try out."

My chin rises in understanding. My sister is a makeup fiend, to put it lightly.

"You stay here. I'll be right back." She unbuckles and exits the car, trotting around it to the sidewalk.

"I don't know about you, but I'm thirsty," Lotus says as he slides out after her.

I shrug. I might as well go inside, too.

Clarity flits up and down the makeup aisle, snatching small, brightly-colored packages from the shelves. Then she turns the corner and grabs several fashion magazines from the metal rack by the row of self-checkout counters, which are manned by one bored-looking teenage boy who is hunched over his phone.

After only a few minutes, Clarity's ready to go and walks up to the first self-checkout kiosk. It looks like the self-checkout counters they used to use a decade ago, except above the computer screen that shows a person's scanned items, there's a black panel—the facial recognition scanner. Every person with a bank account also has their face on file, and banks and commercial businesses all over the world use the database to bill consumers for their purchases.

The store employee, a gangly, bespectacled teen probably about our age, barely looks up from his smart watch as Clarity scans her items with a practiced hand and then stands still in front of the view screen, waiting for it to scan her face. The machine beeps once it's finished, and her banking information comes up on the screen. She hovers over it to shield the information from any possible onlookers, pressing a couple buttons to confirm her purchase.

Lotus strides up to the kiosk beside ours and buys himself a giant energy drink.

Then we pile back into the car to finish the drive home. We pass Foundry Branch Valley Park on the right. It looks like a vast blank space in the dark. We're almost to the hotel now: Darnay Plaza. I roll my eyes. Charles Darnay is a friend of Royal's from the good old days. Apparently he used to be a spy for MI6, but it's really hard to swallow. In the interviews I've seen on TV, he comes across as a mumbling, clumsy ox. Maybe his cover is a dead-on impression of Christopher Reeve's Clark Kent, but without the glasses. Whatever. Royal says he used to be good. And it is nice of Darnay to let us use the secret bunker he built in his hotel here in D.C. Hard to believe he told everyone it was a conference facility. I stifle a snicker. Honestly, people are so gullible.

Lotus maneuvers the car into the hotel parking lot under the building and pulls into a spot in the far corner near the service entrance.

"Everybody out." He exits the car and stands beside it, waiting for Clarity and me.

Clarity picks up the wig box gingerly, clutching it to her chest. I grab the balled-up blouse and my parachute backpack. Then I reach in the car and hand the briefcase to Lotus. "Guard this with your life."

Lotus gives me a sarcastic salute. "Yeah, yeah."

I swing the car door closed and he locks it with the key fob in his hand. We walk through the parking lot, past the service entrance to a metal door in the wall that looks like it hasn't been used in a decade. It has scrapes and dents, and there is rust gathering around the door handle.

Lotus moves to the left of the door and opens the metal casing on what appears to be an electrical box. Inside the panel, there's a flat black screen with a small red light at the top that blinks on and off every few seconds.

Lotus squares himself up to the box and hovers with his face mere inches away from it. The red light turns green and a dull buzz sounds within. Lotus turns the door lever and swings it open. He motions for us to go inside.

We walk into the dimly lit service tunnel that runs under the hotel. Pipes suspended along the ceiling break off in myriad directions.

The cement floor is damp and mossy. It amazes me how humid it is in here even though I walk through this hallway pretty much every day. The garish orange lights that dot the walls make my fair skin glow as bright as a pumpkin. It's not a good look.

At the end of the tunnel we make a left and stand in front of a large concrete door. There's another flat black panel with a blinking red light on the top. This time, Clarity sidles up to the screen and holds still while it scans her face. The door buzzes and disappears into the wall.

We step into the den, which is swathed in a warm glow

cast by industrial-looking steel and glass wall sconces.

Lotus steps to the left to hang his leather jacket on one of the hooks mounted in a row along the wall.

I snag my gray trench coat off another one and drape it over my arm.

Clarity power walks through the den, between the mismatched hotel couches and stuffed chairs, and through the pocket door that leads to the dormitory. She's moving like a bat out of hell, itching to get that wig brushed out, back on its styrofoam head, and in its proper place on the shelf.

"Welcome back." Vale strides toward Lotus and me from the control room, just to our right. He gives Lotus a high five before turning to me. "So? How was it?" he asks in his perfect Alabama accent. His eyes light up as he looks way, way down at me. He's a foot taller than me, which, I admit, is part of the appeal. He grins and his perfectly straight, white teeth glint.

I return the gesture. "Exhilarating. No wonder my grandpa always talked about it."

"I bet." Vale laughs.

"Are you up for a game later?" Lotus asks Vale.

Vale turns to focus on Lotus. "Game?"

"The new Alien Spy game?" Lotus's eyes widen, and he mimics driving a motorcycle with his hands.

"Oh, yeah," Vale says once recognition dawns.

"Awesome. Catch you in a few," Lotus says, moving away from us toward the control room, carrying the briefcase in a steady hand.

Vale turns his haze back to me, stepping closer.

"My grandpa would have liked you," I whisper, brushing my fingers over the skin of his arm.

Vale blushes slightly, a tick Royal has tried to train out of him, to no avail. "Let me help you put all that gear away."

21

"Sure." I tromp past the control room to the armory: a long, narrow space lined with gun safes. I traverse to the far end of the room and open the cage where we keep any non-lethal equipment. I stow my jumping gear, then lay the parachute out to check it over before re-rolling it and tucking it into the pack.

"Let me do that," Vale says, kneeling beside me and taking the parachute from my hands.

"Thanks." I smile as I stand and move to the gun safe I call mine. Putting my hand up to the flat, black screen on the safe's door, I stand still while it reads my palm print. A low beep sounds, and I turn the handle to open the door. I disassemble my tranquilizer gun in a couple quick movements and store the gun and darts in their proper places within the safe. My Glock 19 goes into the safe as well. Only my karambit knives remain hidden in the belt at my waist. Where I go, they go.

"Hey."

I pivot to face Vale, who is standing just behind me, leaning in. "I'm glad you're back safe," he whispers before lowering his lips to mine. His kiss is warm and much too short. He pulls back as I'm reaching up to play with his hair, and looks down the hall toward the control room. There isn't anyone in sight.

I sigh and crane my face up toward his.

He chuckles. "I've gotta finish this parachute first. You go get cleaned up and meet me in the kitchen. I'll make you one of my famous grilled cheeses."

My stomach growls in response. "I *am* pretty hungry."

He nods. "Go on."

"All right." I walk back past the control room and through the den to the dormitory. It's pretty much what you expect when you hear the word: a white hallway filled with six square rooms, their cinder block walls painted white.

I pass Royal's room, which sits across from Vale's right at the mouth of the hall.

The two middle rooms are empty.

Third door on the left is Clarity and me. We've got the option of having our own rooms, but we've shared all our lives and prefer it that way. Photos of fashion icons such as Sophia Loren, Iman, and Emma Watson are taped to the surrounding wall.

Lotus's room is across from ours.

Clarity is there when I enter our room, sitting at her desk, combing out the wavy blonde wig that accompanied me on my jump today. The round, tan-and-white-striped wig box sits open at her feet.

"She needs a shampoo after that jump," Clarity says without looking at me.

I would offer to do it, but Clarity doesn't let anyone else care for her wigs. Her clothes are always scattered over the floor, but her wigs are immaculate rows of color and shape, sitting on foam heads on shelves that span her side of the room.

I pick my way over the mounds of fabric to my side of the room. It's spartan, sterile. It looks mostly abandoned but for the dorm style pine lofted bed with a vintage tanker desk underneath. I pop the tiny, beige comm device out of my ear and leave it sitting alone on top of the metal desk. I slide open the bottom drawer, kiss a finger, and press it to the glass over an old photo of my mom cuddling with an infant me. "Got home safe. Love you," I whisper. It's my ritual after every successful mission. Then I grab a change of clothes from the next drawer up. "I'll be back."

I need a shower. I reek.

Once I'm clean and dressed, I pass through the den and take the stairs down to the kitchen. It's a large room made of concrete, with stainless steel appliances set into the walls. A long, concrete island holds the stovetop and sink. Industrial lamps hang overhead, warming the chilly space.

A long wooden trestle table spans the other side of the room.

I cross to the fridge and pull out butter, fontina, and gorgonzola for my sandwich. The homemade whole wheat loaf sits in the bread box on the counter; a few three-day-old slices are all that remain. Vale hasn't had time to bake a new loaf. I shrug. It'll still be a delicious grilled cheese.

Thumps sound on the stairs down to the kitchen. I lean toward the stairwell and look upward.

Vale is moving down the stairs toward me, wearing a heather gray long sleeved shirt and black knit pants. He beams when he sees me. "Royal went out for a bit."

"Interesting." I back away from him, smiling coyly.

He advances toward me, pinning me against the kitchen counter with his hips, and puts one hand on the counter on each side of me. "What was it you wanted with me?" he drawls, lowering his face toward mine.

"A grilled cheese." I run my hands up his abdomen and over his chest before wrapping them around to rest on his shoulder blades.

"That can be arranged," he whispers in my ear before covering my mouth with his.

The press of his body against mine lights me on fire. I pull him tightly against me. He can't possibly be near enough.

He slides one hand into my trench coat, circling my waist. His hand is warm, his fingers long on the small of my back.

The sound of footsteps on the stairs down to the kitchen reaches our ears and we jump apart. I button up my coat and Vale opens the fridge and leans inside. He'd better get a handle on the flush that covers his face and neck, and quick.

Clarity steps down into the kitchen, her eyes moving between Vale and me. Her mouth twitches, but she says nothing. She meets my gaze, her deep-set brown eyes studying my face.

That was too close. We're getting careless.

I turn toward the cupboard and retrieve three plates. "Clarity? Grilled cheese?"

"Sounds delicious." She smiles as she pulls out a chair facing the kitchen and sits at the table, setting her copy of Zora Neale Hurston down on the wooden surface.

Lotus thumps down into the kitchen. "What's for dinner?"

I snort. "You mean to tell me you didn't eat anything while you were waiting for me in the car?"

A bold smile covers Lotus's face. "Of course I did. This is second dinner. What are we having?"

"Grilled cheeses," Vale says as he pulls back from the fridge. "We've got American, cheddar, fontina, and gorgonzola. Who wants what?"

"The usual for me," I say as I cross the kitchen to sit beside Clarity.

"Traditional American for me." Lotus grins as he pulls out a chair at the end of the table, kitty-corner to Clarity. He leans back in the metal chair and sticks his legs out. "Man it feels good to stretch out. Sitting in that car all day was rough." He looks at Clarity. "Get any reading done today?"

She smiles as she taps her book. "Almost the entire thing."

He shakes his head. "That's amazing."

"I'll have cheddar," Clarity says before picking up her

place in her book.

My watch buzzes. "I'll be back to the Tower in twenty minutes," Royal's voice rises from the watch on my left wrist. "Have everyone assembled in the control room. We've got a new mission."

Chapter 3

"So, sandwiches to go, then?" Vale smiles from where he stands at the stove, and lights a burner. The blue flame flickers as he places the griddle on the cooking surface.

"Sounds like it." I say with a cheshire cat smile. I'm still excited after my jump, and a new job sounds amazing.

"Come help slice some cheese, will you?" Vale gives me a crooked smile over the stove, unwrapping a slice of American cheese as he looks at me. He makes taking plastic wrap off cheese slices look oh so sexy. I stand and cross the room toward him, rolling up the sleeves of my trench coat so I can work. I retrieve the cheese slicer from under the cabinet and brush past Vale, allowing my hand to swipe across his butt as I do so. Then I get to work cutting the fontina. I steal a glance at him as I work. Red has crept up his neck to his cheeks again. I bite my lip to suppress a smirk. He's so easy to embarrass.

"So Lotus, when is the old man going to let you try flying again?" Vale asks without looking up from the grilled cheese sandwich that's sizzling on the griddle. He holds the flat, slotted spatula in his hand, poised to flip the crackling sandwich once it's reached a greasy, golden brown color.

Lotus laughs. "I don't know. I scared him pretty good last

time. I need to do a few more runs on the simulator before I ask about it." He scratches the black stubble on his chin as he gazes across the room not looking at anything in particular. "It sure would be awesome to get my pilot's license though."

"You'll get there." Clarity pats Lotus's arm without looking up from her book.

"Thanks, C." Lotus pulls out his phone and starts scrolling. "I've been looking at planes. I'd love to get into the cockpit of a Cessna Citation X. Those things can move." He grins to himself.

"Maybe someday," I say, "we'll need one for a mission."

"That would be the dream," he says.

Unlike Lotus, I don't carry a phone anymore. I had become so addicted to it, I almost missed a money drop in the middle of a ransom situation. It was a wake-up call that made me aware of how the phone dulled my senses, making my mental reckoning sluggish. Now, if I need to carry a phone for a job, it's a dumb one that is only capable of phone calls and messaging. I feel much freer without it. My mind is clearer and quicker on the uptake.

"One pile of freshly sliced cheese, coming up." I run my finger along the wire to catch any remaining cheese residue and lick it off my finger. Then I slide the plate of sliced, creamy goodness over to Vale. He lays it over a slice of bread, adds some Gorgonzola, and smears a pat of butter on the griddle before adding my sandwich. The smell of melting cheese fills the kitchen and makes my stomach growl.

Vale's green eyes meet mine and we're locked in place, the heat between us crackling, making me run my tongue over my upper lip.

From the table, Clarity lets out a single cough.

My head snaps up and I look at her, but her eyes haven't

lifted from her novel. She didn't see.

I turn back to Vale. "Thanks for making these," I say before retreating to the table. I've got to get myself in check. There is no way that Clarity and Lotus can find out about us. Clarity could keep a secret, but Lotus? Not a chance. He'd get to talking with Royal and it would slip out before his mind could catch up.

"My pleasure," Vale says, his southern drawl more pronounced. I've noticed it comes out when he's doing domestic tasks. He says it's because they remind him of being home with his parents in Alabama. He doesn't see them much now; our hectic schedule doesn't permit visits home. Luckily for me, my dad and adopted sister live right here in the Ivory Tower.

Vale finishes making his and Lotus's sandwiches and carries them over to us.

"Thanks man, it looks great." Lotus picks his up and takes a huge bite.

I stand, plate in hand. "Let's head to the control room." I glance down at my watch. "Royal should be back by now."

Clarity folds down one corner of the page she is reading before closing her book and standing in one fluid motion. She picks up her sandwich and leads the way up the stairs toward the control room. Lotus follows her, and then Vale. I bring up the rear, flipping the lights off on my way out.

We move through the den to the control room and take seats at the long metal table near the back wall. It's where we usually sit to receive our instructions for new missions and to debrief about old ones. The room isn't what you would expect based on the movies. It's not all high tech, invisible computer screens and giant countdown clocks. In reality, it's nothing but a regular office with a couple desks and computers. There are no papers at all. We don't bother with them anymore—we memorize what we need to know. There are two wooden desks toward the front of the room, each with a closed laptop on their surface. Beyond that, a large monitor hangs on the front wall. At the moment, it's not on.

Lotus sits in a chair and chows down on his sandwich, making small noises of delight as he eats.

Clarity takes dainty bites between page flips, reading as quickly as her eyes can scan the page.

Vale sits next to me and touches my shoe with his under the table. I give him a tap back in response before digging into my own sandwich.

Royal, my and Clarity's dad, walks in five minutes later, his navy suit and maroon button-up shirt still crisp, even though he's been in them for hours. He sets his laptop bag down on one of the desks and unfastens the button nearest his collar before turning to face us. "From what I've heard so far, it looks like you did a stellar job, Loveday. I'm proud."

"Thanks, Royal. I loved every minute of it."

"That's my girl." Royal grins at me. We are cut from the same cloth, he and I. He runs a hand through his brown hair graying at the temples, then taps his watch with one hand.

The ping of an incoming air drop draws my eyes to my watch. An image of a hotel lights up the large screen. My eyes widen when I see the name of the hotel. "Darnay Plaza in London?"

Clarity nearly drops her book. "Are we going to London?"

Royal nods. "We are indeed. Charles himself has asked us to come and help them with a security matter at his hotels there. It should be a pretty easy assignment, and we'll make some time to visit some historical sights once we're done. I know Loveday is the only one of you who has ever been to

London."

"I was one. I don't remember anything about it." I'm smiling. I can't wait to hop on the plane.

"London, huh? Sounds awesome." Lotus grins.

Clarity bites her lip. "Do you think we will have time to visit Sicily?"

Royal nods. "I don't see why not."

Clarity beams and skips across the control room to give him a hug. "Thanks, Dad!"

He gives her a squeeze before letting go. "Happy to." He looks over at the rest of us. "We leave at 0400, so I suggest you pack tonight. Oh, and I know the drinking age over there is 18, but don't even think about it." He levies an icy blue stare at Vale and Lotus, who at 18 and 19 are the only ones of age. Clarity and I are both are only 17 and change.

"This is a work trip," Royal continues. "We must be alert, precise. This is not the time for sloppiness."

"Yes, sir," Vale says.

Lotus gives an exaggerated salute.

Royal makes a show of rolling his eyes. "Oh, knock it off." He retrieves our passports from his jacket pocket and holds them up. "You'll be traveling under fake names, so memorize the details in these."

"What names did you choose?" I ask, striding toward him with my eyes narrowed suspiciously. It would be like him to put ridiculous names on our passports, like Pansy Picklebottom or John Johns, just to mess with us.

Royal's blue eyes pierce. "What types of names do you think I should have chosen?"

I reach out for the passports, but he holds them higher, out of my reach.

I take a step back, arms across my chest. "Common,

boring names, so we don't stand out."

He nods, lowering the travel documents so I can retrieve them. Flipping through them confirms my hunch: each of us has been assigned a conventional, ho-hum name. "Not bad."

Royal scratches his nose. "For you, I considered Ezmeralda Frankenbush."

"Right." I shake my head at him before turning to my teammates and handing over their passports. The energy in the room spikes. This is getting more real by the minute.

Clarity hunches over Lotus's shoulder, reading the information in his passport. "Tyler Williams. Isn't that the name of an actor?"

Lotus nods. "Yep."

"Why not travel under our real names?" Vale asks, open passport in hand.

"As you know, our policy is never to share such personal, identifying traits with each other." Royal catches each of our gazes in turn. "That might sound extreme, but it'll keep you safe if something goes wrong." His mouth forms a tight line. Missions have gone wrong for my dad more than once. At least, that's an assumption I make, because he won't tell me.

My body buzzes with energy, but I work to remain composed. Dad expects me to lead by example; I can't allow the giddiness building in me to surface. This will be our first international mission, and even though Charles Darnay is involved, I have a great feeling about it. Thankfully, unlike Vale, my poker face is as impenetrable as tungsten carbide.

"Sir?" Vale asks, voice tentative. "Can I tell my... everyone at home that we're going to Europe? So they don't worry if I don't have time to call them?"

In my excitement, it hasn't even occurred to me that Vale has parents back home who will miss him if he doesn't make their weekly phone call. He's the only one of us who has family outside the Tower. I cock my head toward Royal, curious to see what he'll say.

"No. You can tell them we're going out of the country, but no more than that."

I'm not surprised. Military personnel who are deployed to certain areas aren't allowed to tell their loved ones where they're headed either. Unlike them, we aren't going into a warzone, but as spies, we still have to stay under the radar. Plus, you never know when someone is listening.

Vale nods. "Thanks." He leaves the room at a brisk pace.

"Go on, then. Get your gear together." Royal waves us off and, taking his laptop, steps into the small alcove off the control room that serves as his office, closing the door behind him.

"You heard him," I say, putting a hand on Clarity's shoulder. "Let's start packing." As team leader, it's my job to keep everyone on track, but most of the time it's not necessary. This moment is a good example of that.

In her excitement, Clarity nearly skips off down the hall, and Lotus follows her, trying to chat with her about London.

I knock on Royal's office door.

"Yes?" he says from within, his voice cool and composed.

I swing the door open and smile at my dad. He's sitting at his desk, which was constructed out of a 4' portion of the wing of his first airplane: a Cessna 172 that he bought thirty years ago. It's got small dings and scrapes, which is pretty cool. The blemishes in the metal catch my eye. I'd love to hear stories of how the plane got so battered: what missions he went on, what adventures he was having when each of those marks appeared. He's tight-lipped about it, of course, since most of that information is classified property of the CIA.

His blue eyes light up. "I'm looking forward to seeing how you and the team do in London. It'll be quite a change from working here."

I turn to study the map of Washington, D.C., that covers one wall of the control room. My eyes land on the spot where our hotel sits, although there is no indication of it on the map. It's the only art on the otherwise bare walls. "I know it." I meet my dad's eyes. "We're ready." I am ready.

He studies me without blinking, before lifting the corners of his mouth. "Your cool head during your flight earlier showed me that you are. Want to make the drop off?"

My eyes widen. He's never let me deliver goods to a client before, even though I'm our team leader. He always does it himself. "Definitely. Yes."

He nods. "Put on something that makes you look like a bike messenger. Take Lotus's bike and helmet. I'll send you the address."

"Yes, sir." I spin on my heel and march through the den toward the dormitory. Adrenaline courses through me. My first drop off! This is going to be—"

Fingers wrap around my wrist and pull me into Vale's room, shutting the door behind us. In an instant Vale is pressed up against me, craning his neck downward to cover my lips with his own. His arms tighten around me as his hands glide up my back inside my trench coat. I fling my arms around his neck and pull him in tighter, running one hand through his wavy brunette hair. My entire body goes up in flames.

Vale's mouth travels down to my jawline, and a nibble on my ear makes my neck tingle.

I turn my head to find his mouth again, but his whisper stops me.

"Want to meet me in the shower in five minutes?" He is

breathing heavily.

I push back the fog of lust that clouds my mind. I can't, but damn I want to.

I focus on the pressure of Vale's large hands on my back before responding. "Royal's letting me make the drop tonight." I drop my hands from Vale's neck and turn my face toward his to give him a peck on the lips. The flush of his skin covers his face and neck, making him look overheated from exertion. I flick at his chin with my nose.

Vale sighs deeply before taking a step back from me. "That's great." He holds his hands down over his front and clears his throat. "You'd better get going."

"Continue later?" I wiggle my eyebrows at him.

He nods. "Yeah."

I give him a smile before opening the door and peeking down the hallway. Lotus's door is open, and so is the door to the room I share with Clarity, but the music coming from Lotus's room is loud enough to drown out incidental noises. Like the surprised squeak I made when Vale's fingers found my wrist. I shut Vale's door noiselessly and cross the hall to my room.

Clarity sits cross-legged on her mattress, which lays on the floor beside her vanity. She got rid of her bed frame when it was clear she needed more shelves for her wigs. She's deep in concentration, practicing a complex braid on a long, silky silver-gray wig. "Come here. I want to try something." She beckons me forward without looking up.

"Can't," I say. "Royal's letting me do the drop off." A grin rises to my lips.

Her eyes fly up to meet mine. "That's amazing. What's the brief?"

"Bike messenger," I say, running my fingers through my

hair. I dig a pair of athletic shorts, a sports bra, and a loose tee out of my dresser and change quickly. "I'll be back in a bit." I give Clarity a quick kiss on the cheek, and then cross to Lotus's room.

His bed is lofted on one side of the room, with his desk below, just like mine. On the other there's an old two-seater sofa facing a small television. A couple of game consoles are stacked in the cabinet underneath it and there's a controller on the floor. Above the TV there's a shelf with half a dozen shot glasses from cities we've visited, mostly around the eastern half of the country. We're not old enough to use them, but Lotus says he'll throw us a giant party when we're all finally of age. He's got a few years to wait.

Lotus is on the floor doing pushups. A grunt escapes him as he completes one. "Hey," he rasps. "What's up?"

"How many have you done?" I sidle up to him and watch. "47… 48… 49… 50."

"Want some extra resistance?" I laugh as I swing one leg over him and plop down on his back.

"No!" Lotus lowers himself to the ground, arms trembling. "Get off me," he chuckles but doesn't move.

"Now that I've got you here, I demand use of your bicycle and helmet."

"Anything you want. Just get off me."

I scoff. "I'm not that heavy."

"Experience tells me I shouldn't respond to that."

I pat his short curly afro before standing. "Good boy. Royal's letting me make the drop, which is why I need the bike."

Lotus rolls over and rests his head on his hands, elbows out wide. "Awesome. Good luck. And seriously, take whatever you need."

I nod. "Thanks, Bro."

He rolls his eyes, but a smirk rises to his lips. "I'm not your bro."

"Whatever you say."

I traipse down the hall into the den. Lotus is right; he's not really my brother. Three years ago, Lotus was busted for joyriding for a fourth time and moved from foster care to a juvenile detention center. We were in need of a driver, so when my dad got wind of his escapades, he put him in training, and brought him here. Royal offered to adopt him as he had Clarity, but Lotus declined. He said he didn't need a piece of paper to tell him where he belonged. So, no, he's not technically my brother. He just feels like one.

I walk into the control room and knock on Royal's office door.

"Come in, Loveday." His voice emanates from behind the metal door, which is open a sliver. The jaunty sounds of the *Pirates of the Caribbean* soundtrack flow from the speakers on his laptop. It's an obsession of his. I'm tempted to ask him about the subsequent films and get him ranting—it's one of the only things he rants about, ever—but now isn't the time.

He picks up a small, padded mailer and holds it out to me.

I turn it over to look at the address: XCom, Oak Street, Arlington, Virginia

My mouth breaks into a wide smile. "I get to bike across the bridge? Sweet."

Royal grins. "It's a great ride. Only about ten minutes."

"Thank you for this." I'm so elated I reach out and give him a side hug, which ends up feeling a little awkward. We're not big on touchy feelings in this family, except for Clarity.

I don my gray leather jacket, pluck Lotus's helmet off one of the hooks in the den, and exit through the service tunnel.

My watch beeps just as I'm mounting Lotus's bike in the underground parking garage.

Vale
Have fun, gorgeous.

My exterior is cool as a cucumber, but my insides heat and my heart speeds up. I delete the message. I can't afford to leave evidence like that somewhere anyone could see it. Vale really shouldn't send me notes on our watches like that. If Royal decided to go through them, for whatever reason, he'd be in for some scintillating reading. Then, Vale and I would be in deep, deep trouble.

I throw my leg over the bike and pedal out of the parking garage and down the street. The hotel backs up to the edge of the park, a drainage ditch is the only barrier between the hotel's small, above-ground valet parking lot and the lush, wooded area. Beyond the trees, there's a killer view of the city. I often see deer in the park when I go for runs on early mornings. But I don't get to do it super often, because most of our missions take place late at night. What they say is true: a lot goes on after the sun goes down. That's when the cockroaches of the world scuttle out into the open and conduct their business, spreading their diseases.

That's where we come in—Royal, Lotus, Vale, Clarity, and myself. We cut off the cockroaches' heads before they have a chance to complete their work.

I ride through the tree-lined streets, which are well lit by towering streetlights and the flashes of car headlights. It's late, but there are still quite a few cars out.

The ride across the bridge is quick but exhilarating. I take the walking path on the eastern side of the bridge. There aren't any pedestrians on it now, so I pump my legs, pushing my limit to see how fast I can travel on the bike. My watch is pressed to my wrist, keeping track of my heart rate and rate of travel. The water at my side is inky black, its movements only hinted at by the sparkles of light that catch its surface.

I pedal down Oak Street and stop in front of XCom. The building must be twenty stories high, paneled in tinted glass. A few office lights dot the edifice, but most of the building is shrouded in darkness.

I park my bike and walk up to the front door, jiggling the handle. It doesn't budge. Movement inside the building catches my eye. A guard is approaching the door, his fit frame noticeable in his tailored black suit.

My eyebrows raise. He is definitely not a run-of-the-mill rent-a-cop like I'm used to seeing on after-hours security detail.

"Do you have the package?" he asks through the locked door.

I hold it up so he can see the address written on the outside, not saying anything.

The security guard unlocks the door and opens it just wide enough to allow me to slide the padded envelope through into his waiting hand.

He nods and closes the door, locking it. Beyond him, the security desk is the only area of the lobby that's still lit. He rounds the counter and stands, watching me carefully.

I hop on my bike and pedal back toward the hotel, my mind on high alert.

I'm crossing the bridge when the screech of car tires grinding against concrete fills my ears. I whip around just in time to see a car slamming into the outer guard rail. A thread of smoke wafts up from the engine of the car, and an image fills my mind. A car crumpled against a tree, front airbags filling the cabin, sprinkled with shards of glass from the shattered windshield. A woman slumped in the driver's seat, her face bloodied. An 18-month-old baby wailing in the back seat, restrained by the straps of her car seat. The night my mother died.

Chapter 4

I make a quick turn and race toward the smoking car. I'm there in a couple seconds, just as another car pulls to the side of the road and the driver steps out.

"Call 911," I yell as I rush toward the crashed vehicle and yank open the driver's side door. It's an elderly woman, the papery skin on her arms a rash of red from contact with the airbag. Dark red blood is oozing from her mouth.

She mumbles something, but I can't make it out. "Let's get you out of the car," I say in a steady, reassuring voice as I reach across her and unbuckle her seatbelt.

She grips my forearm, and together we manage to get her into a standing position. I lead her a few yards past the front of her car and ease her to a seated position. Traffic is completely stopped on this side of the bridge, so I'm not worried about someone hitting us accidentally.

Loud, wailing sirens close in on our location and an ambulance pulls up. The EMTs hop out of their van and flank the woman, encouraging her to try to speak to them. One looks up and meets my eyes. "What happened?" she asks.

"I don't know. All I saw was her car hitting the guardrail."

The man I told to call 911 steps forward. "I saw it all," he says, and the EMT gives him a faint smile. I wait until they're conversing about the crash to fade into the clump of motorists who have stopped their cars on this side of the bridge and climbed out of their cars to look. Tiptoeing back to my bike, I hightail it back to the Ivory Tower before anything else happens.

Clarity, Lotus, and Vale are sitting on the floor, hovering over an old Monopoly game when I step inside. Clarity sits at one end of the board, her legs folded to one side underneath her, wearing her usual olive green slacks and a cream-colored button-up blouse.

Lotus sits across from her in his red basketball shorts and black tank.

Vale sits between them in a heather gray tee and black knit pants.

We each have a sort of uniform that we wear around the Tower. It helps us separate our reality here in the Tower from the roles we play outside these walls. Without it, it would be much harder to compartmentalize our work from life outside the job. Our clothing is a visual cue that we're home safe and acting as our true selves.

"Join us," Clarity says, her eyes gleaming. "We're taking a break from packing."

"Speak for yourself," Lotus says.

Vale points a finger at her. "She's taking a break. We're pretty much done."

Clarity titters. My sister and her board games. But then she catches sight of me and her mouth drops. "What happened?" She's on me in a second, pawing all over me.

"What are you doing?" I ask as I try to push her away.

"You've got blood all over you."

At this, Vale hops up and comes over, concern in his eyes.

I look down, and sure enough there is blood smeared on the front of my shirt. "Oh, it's not mine. I'm fine."

"Whose is it?" Vale asks, eyeing me. "Did the drop go badly?"

"No!" I burst out. "It went fine."

"You sure?" Lotus asks over Clarity's shoulder.

"Yeah. I'm sure. After I made the drop, there was a car accident. I helped the driver out of the car. A little old lady."

"Oh. Is she going to be okay?" Clarity asks, her hand still on my arm.

"I think so."

"Thank goodness." She gives me a squeeze and goes back to her spot at the game board. "Get changed and come play with us."

"Yeah. If we have to play, so do you." Lotus shakes his head, feigning annoyance. But a subtle smile plays on his mouth as he leans back against the couch. He loves it too. It's much better than the every-man-for-himself mentality he encountered in the group home he lived in before Royal brought him here. He hasn't said much about it, per Royal's gag order on personal information, but I've picked up the hints Lotus has dropped.

Vale beckons with one hand for me to come over.

I hang Lotus's helmet on a hook by the door to the service tunnel. "Let me change first."

"Hurry up," Lotus says.

I jog down the dormitory hall and into our room, tossing my athletic gear in the small clothes hamper under my lofted bed and donning my uniform: black tee, black leggings, belt with karambits securely in place, and warm, fuzzy black socks. I drape my trench coat over my shoulders but don't put my arms through the holes. I close my eyes and listen to the sounds in the Tower: the faint, brassy sounds of Royal's film soundtrack, the low hum of the lights strung down the hallway, the chatter of my friends in the den. I breathe in deeply through my nose and let it out slowly through my mouth. Then again. A quick kiss to my mom, and then I'm off down the hall.

"Those guys at XCom don't mess around," I say as I plop down on the floor between Clarity and Lotus. I meet Vale's eyes for a second before turning to Clarity. "The night security guard was not your average mall cop."

Clarity's eyes widen. "What do you mean?"

"Well, for starters he had a gun instead of a baton. Beretta 92C. He didn't take his hand off it the entire time the door was unlocked."

"I'm not surprised," Vale says. "They've got to protect their facial recognition software."

Lotus leans forward. "Did they...?"

"Invent the facial recognition software that pretty much every company in the world uses for their payment system? Yeah." Vale rubs the scruff on his chin. "Lots of people would pay a ton to get their hands on it."

Lotus turns to me. "What did you give them?"

I shrug. "I didn't ask."

"You don't know?"

"I trust Royal, so it doesn't matter what it was."

"This is the first time he's let one of us make the drop off, so it can't have been dangerous," Clarity says as she sorts the Monopoly money into neat piles by denomination. "Everyone pick a token."

Vale catches my eye and smiles. "Try not to cheat this time."

I smirk right back. "It wasn't cheating. You weren't paying

attention."

He points a finger at me. "You landed on my property and didn't pay the rent."

"You snooze, you lose."

"Okay, children," Lotus interrupts. "Let's get this started."

But I do cheat, every chance I get. Partly because it's hilarious when Vale or Lotus misses it—though Clarity never does—and partly because within these walls, I'm betting with paper money and losing only results in some friendly mocking from my teammates. Outside these walls, the money is real, and the stakes are forever.

Chapter 5

"I win." I grin as I collect Clarity's money. She's the last of my opponents to declare bankruptcy. The boys were out ages ago due to their lack of observational skills.

"I'll have to pay more attention next time," Vale drawls, his light green eyes meeting my own.

"Next time? I'm not playing with this cheater again for a while." Lotus tosses his mortgaged property cards at me and stands. His eyes fall to his watch. "It's late, folks. We'd better finish packing."

"I can't decide which wigs to bring," Clarity breathes as she stacks the cards and puts them haphazardly into the game box. She floats across the room and slides the box into the console table under the flat screen TV.

"How many do you need?" Vale studies her as she moves toward us.

Clarity brings her fingers up to her lips. "If I knew how many days we'd be gone…"

I stand. "Come on. I'll help you decide."

Clarity beams as she slides an arm across my shoulders and leans her head down to rest against mine. It makes me feel small, safe. It's one positive about being six inches shorter than her, despite being several months older. "Night," Clarity says to Vale before steering me toward the dormitory.

"Night," he calls to us.

I don't dare glance back at him. It's a miracle Clarity hasn't picked up on our vibes yet, and I have to keep it that way.

Uneven snoring emits from Royal's room as we pass. He slipped past us and went to bed hours ago, which is probably for the best since he's not capable of sleeping on planes. Never has been. I, on the other hand, can sleep anywhere. It's a gift, really.

We walk into our room and Clarity flicks on the light.

My eyes are drawn to the wooden shelves that run the length of the wall on her side of the room, each one lined with Styrofoam heads bearing different identities she and I have both crawled into at one point or another, like slipping on another layer of skin that allows us to hide in plain sight until our work is done. When we're finished, we crawl back into our cave and shed that skin, much like a snake would. Only instead of a cave, we return to the Ivory Tower.

I sigh, not taking my eyes from the strokes and swirls of color along Clarity's walls. "Who do you want to be in London? A librarian?" I point to a brunette wig with a blunt lob cut and full bangs. "A mermaid?" This time I point to a waist-length, curly, seaweed-green wig.

She taps her lip with her pointer, resting her other hand in the crook of her elbow. After a moment, she steps forward and brings down a straight, deep burgundy wig that falls to her shoulder blades. "Maybe something in between?"

My fingers brush through the thick, soft wig. "I love that one."

She smiles and hands it to me so she can retrieve the zippered wig box she keeps under her vanity. "Now, which one

47

should I wear on the plane?"

It takes us a while to pack all of Clarity's stuff; her wigs, makeup, and eclectic wardrobe choices take up two suitcases. I pick out a couple of wigs for her to bring for me, just in case, bringing the total to eight.

Packing my things is much easier. I toss in three pairs of black jeggings, five black tees, a bunch of socks, underwear, bralettes, and toiletries, and I'm good to go.

"Bring a swimsuit too," Clarity chirps. She holds up her red and white floral high-waisted bikini. "You never know!"

I cock my head. "We *are* staying in a pretty fancy hotel…"

"Did I hear something about swimsuits?" Vale pops his head in the door.

Clarity grins, showing off her pearly white teeth. "Were you spying on us?"

"No self-respecting southern gentleman would ever be caught spying." He winks.

"That wasn't a denial." I smirk, placing one hand on my hip.

Vale laughs. "I was just coming to ask what you girls are bringing for entertainment on the plane."

Clarity holds up a copy of *The Fountainhead*. "Books, Darling."

Vale's eyes lock on me. "And you, Loveday?" he asks.

"Books?" I smile. "Seriously, though, I'm planning on sleeping the whole time."

"Speaking of." Vale stretches, raising his arms into the air, making me very aware of his long, lean body and muscled arms.

I give myself a mental shake to regain focus.

"Good night." Vale smiles at us before ducking back into the hallway.

Without a word I dig my black bikini out of the drawer

and stuff it into my duffel bag. Maybe Vale and I will finally find some alone time on this trip; we are staying at a luxury hotel in London, after all, instead of a concrete bunker. I glance at Clarity, who has gone back to fussing with her wigs. It's a wonder she doesn't suspect.

Chapter 6

"Hey," Vale says when he finds me in one of the two dormitory bathrooms at 03:30. He walks up to where I'm standing at the sink, washing my face. I'm hoping the scrubbing will help me wake up, but it's not cutting it. Two hours of sleep isn't even close to being enough.

"Hey," I say, flicking my eyes to his face before returning my focus to the mirror.

Vale sets his razor down on the edge of the sink and watches me, arms crossed.

I can't help but laugh. "Is there a reason you're hovering instead of using the other bathroom?"

"Clarity's in there. Door's locked."

"Oh." I raise my eyebrows. If Clarity's in there, it's going to be a while. She often locks herself into the bathroom to try out a new look, especially when she wants to surprise us. Last time she did that she came out looking exactly like me, only taller and much tanner. On contact with the sun, my fair skin simply freckles. "I'm almost done here."

Vale smiles. "You ready for London?"

"Hell yes. I haven't been abroad in years. My passport is embarrassingly empty for a supposed professional snoop."

A low chuckle erupts from Vale's throat. "You are something else, Love."

I go still. He only calls me that when we're alone, obviously, but this time it carries an undercurrent. I know where this is going.

Vale leans toward me and nibbles at my neck.

The tickling makes me scrunch my shoulders up toward my ears. "Let me finish washing my face first."

"All right."

He rests against the wall and waits while I rinse my face and pat dry. It's hard to pull my eyes away from his snug, white undershirt and pajama shorts.

I pat my face dry and hang the towel on a hook on the wall next to the sink. I close the distance between us and wrap my arms around his torso, pressing my face into his chest, and let out a deep sigh. "Maybe we can sneak off at some point while we're in London. Just the two of us."

Vale runs a hand up and down my back slowly as he rests his chin on the top of my head. "Maybe we won't have to sneak at all."

I pull back and look up to meet his face. "What do you mean?"

He bites his lip before responding. "I think we should tell your dad about us."

I rear back, dropping my arms to my sides. "What? Not a chance. He'd send you away like that." I snap to emphasize my point.

Vale shakes his head. "I don't think so. We haven't allowed it to affect our performance. He'll see that."

I cross my arms. "It doesn't matter. He'll make the argument that it's only because things are going well. Once we have a fight or something..." My voice trails off.

He sounds so sure, so confident when he says, "We won't."

My brows scrunch together. "You can't know that. Everyone fights sometime."

"You and Clarity don't."

I cross my arms. "That's different."

"Please, Love. I'm tired of hiding how I feel about you when we're around everyone else. It would feel so good to be able to hold your hand out in public."

I square my jaw. "No. We can't tell him. I won't do it."

A weary sigh escapes from Vale's lips. "Fine." He turns toward the mirror and starts to shave his stubble, holding his skin taut as he moves the razor.

"Vale…" I put one hand on his back, but he doesn't turn. "Maybe if this job goes well. Maybe when we get back." But my heart isn't in it. I never want to tell Royal about Vale and me, and the steely look in Vale's eyes tells me that he knows it.

I leave the bathroom, shutting the door behind me. A weight settles in my chest. We can't tell Royal about us; he'll completely flip out. Plus, he'd bench one or both of us using the argument that our judgment is compromised. Like hell it is.

Chapter 7

I'm excited. Darnay sprung for first-class seats for our entire team. But even so, I keep it bottled up where no one else can see it. As our team leader, I have to remain calm, collected, in control. I may be doing cartwheels on the inside, but on the outside, I'm all business. Despite Clarity's patient coaching, I could never figure out how to do cartwheels anyway. Maybe jumping jacks. Those I can handle.

We're spread out in our black fifteen-passenger van as it rumbles toward the airport with Royal at the wheel. Lotus sits up front with him, his head cushioned on the jacket he has balled up against the window.

Vale is upright in his seat, alone in the middle row, his wavy dark brown hair mussed. His navy hoodie is bunched up, but he doesn't seem to mind. His earbuds are in place. The faint sounds of heavy metal music reach my ears. I cringe. Vale put it on in the car's stereo system once, but Royal only made it through the first ten seconds before groaning and turning it off. I have to say, I'm Team Royal on this one. I don't get the appeal.

Since our conversation in the bathroom, Vale hasn't said more than a couple words to me. He wants to be honest with our team—my family—but I'm positive it won't go how he thinks it will. Frankly, I'm surprised we've gotten away with it for this long. Four months is a long time to hide a romantic relationship from people, especially Clarity. She doesn't miss much. In fact, there have been a couple of times when I thought she was going to ask me about Vale, but she hasn't. It's only a matter of time until she does.

I twist around to look at my sister. She's in the row behind me, sprawled out in the seat with a u-shaped cushion around her neck and a blanket around her legs and torso. She chose a brunette pixie wig for the flight, which surprised me. It's the tamest wig she's ever worn for a trip. In the past, rainbow waves or stick-straight neon blue was more her style. Instead, the sleek, dark brown locks of her wig float around her ears, making her look younger than she is, her square face framed by dark fringe. She's got a sleeping mask over her eyes, her body still except for the undulations that come with being in a moving car.

The van hits a pothole and Clarity jolts before raising her mask to reveal one eye. She sits up to look over the interior of the van, and, once satisfied she's not missing anything, replaces the mask.

I look down at the book I've got clutched in my hands. It's a green, cloth-bound copy of *A Little Princess*, one of my mother's books. I open it to study the ink and watercolor illustrations at the beginning of each chapter, their brush strokes and ink spots as familiar to me as Royal's cool blue eyes or Clarity's glittering brown ones, but it's still too dark out to do any reading. I close the book and set it on the seat beside me. Rolling my head back and forth against the headrest allows me to find the most comfortable position. Unlit buildings move up the sidewalk as we pass. We'll be at the airport soon enough.

"This is unbelievable." Lotus chortles, one hand over his mouth as we are led into the first-class compartment of the plane. "I can't believe this."

"That's what unbelievable means," I say, reaching out to poke Lotus in the back, but I'm grinning too. It's fantastic; it's so much better than coach, which is all I've ever flown until today. A lot can be said about Charles Darnay—most of it less than stellar—but I have to say, it was really solid of him to spring for five first class tickets for our flight to London.

Lotus swats me away, his eyes wide as he takes in the three spacious rows of individual cubicles, each equipped with a fully reclining chair, mini television, cup holder, a small desk, and a tiny brass lamp.

Vale skirts past me, trying to suck in as he moves so he won't jostle me much. His hand brushes my arm, and then his back is to me as he walks up the aisle. My eyes follow him, unsure if the touch was intentional.

The flight attendant, cheery in his crisp, black slacks and gray button-down shirt, leads Lotus and Vale up the aisle to their seats in the middle row, and then escorts Clarity and me to ours. "Is it your first time flying first class?" he asks with a smile.

"Yes." Clarity nods.

"Oh yeah," I say.

"Then you're in for a treat." He shows us the features of our individual cubbies, complete with a sleeping mask, access to hundreds of movies and television shows, and a menu of foods we can order at any time during our flight. There's even a dividing wall between my cubby and Clarity's that can be raised or lowered. My eyes almost pop out of my head, but I blink a few times in rapid succession in an effort to remain focused. This is not the time to squeal about our accommodations.

We're embarking on our first international mission and we have to be on point the entire time. There is no room for mistakes.

I'm cozy in my seat, flicking through the options on the television when the dividing wall beside me lowers.

"Hey," Clarity whispers, leaning toward me. "Isn't this fantastic?" Her smile spreads from ear to ear, and the warm glow of the sunrise flares through the window behind her, catching her hair and setting it aglow.

I smile in return. "It's pretty great." I set the remote down and turn toward her. She needs to know I'm focused on her and not the Marvel movie I've just started. It's something Royal does, gives his full attention to the person he's talking to, and I try to do the same. In my line of work it's important to support and encourage my teammates, because one day they may be the thin line between success and serious injury, or worse.

"Have you seen this breakfast menu? What are you going to order?" She holds up the laminated page so I can see it.

"Hmm, let me find mine." I rummage around my cubby and my fingers run over the pouch that's secured to the inside edge of my chair where only I can reach it. I scan over the menu quickly until my eyes land on an item I can't pass up.

"So?" Clarity prompts.

"Lobster roll." The thought of a warm, butter-soaked roll stuffed with lobster makes my stomach growl. A smile plays on my lips. I would consider killing for shellfish. We don't get a lot of it in the Tower. Every once in a while Royal treats us to dinner at the swanky hotel restaurant and allows us to order whatever we want, but mostly we eat much more basic fare back at the Tower since we all take turns cooking. Vale does a majority of the food prep, although Clarity enjoys doing it on occasion. Lotus and I are pretty useless in the kitchen as anything more than assistants.

"I'm going with smoked salmon eggs benedict."

"That sounds amazing. You'll have to let me try it."

"Yes, ma'am." She gives me a salute.

Laughter bubbles up in me. I *am* excited about this trip, and I'm thrilled to have this time with my sister. We don't get a lot of alone time, even though we share the same room. I breathe in deeply, savoring this moment. Because when we step off the plane in London, it's game on.

Chapter 8

Two Marvel movies later, the almost eight hour flight is going by much more quickly than I would have imagined, and I haven't had a chance to talk to Vale. The first time I walked up the aisle toward his seat, using the pretense that I had to use the restroom, he was deep in conversation with Lotus. The second time I got a suspicious look from Clarity, and it wasn't worth it because Vale was asleep. Now, he and Lotus are having a *Fast and Furious* marathon. Vale's still wearing his navy hoodie, but now it's pulled up to cover his head. I shiver. It's cold in the plane cabin. I retrieve my trench coat from where it's balled up at my feet, stand, and put it on. I button up the front and pop the collar so it circles my neck.

Out of the corner of my eye, I see Lotus making his way toward the bathroom at the front of the cabin.

"Going somewhere?" Clarity asks as she removes an earbud from her ear, her brown eyes looking up at me full of questions. A map of London glows on the screen of the tablet resting in her lap. She loves maps, my sister, and always studies the layout of the cities we visit before we arrive. It's come in handy more than once.

"Bathroom," I say. "Be right back."

"Again?" My sister's voice is edged with disbelief.

"Too much sparkling water," I say, and start walking before she can ask any more questions. Once I'm a few rows up, I look back. Clarity has settled back down in her seat and replaced the wireless earbuds through which she's listening to an audiobook while she uses her tablet.

I walk slowly up the aisle, making sure of my footing with each step, eyes scanning the passengers for anything out of the ordinary. The woman in the compartment behind Vale is hooked on a movie, her earbuds in her ears. The man beside Vale is asleep, snuggled under a blanket. Royal is in a seat at the front of the cabin, reading something on his laptop. Perfect.

I slide into Lotus's cubby and sit, leaning toward Vale and waiting until he turns to me, making eye contact.

He reaches up and takes out his earbuds, eyes wary. "What's up?"

"I can't stay long. I just wanted to talk to you."

Vale nods slowly. "What about?"

There is no sign of Lotus, and Royal is still reading, so I reach over the lowered cubby divider and take Vale's hand in mine. "Are we okay?"

His eyes sink to the floor.

I frown. "I guess that answers that question."

Vale sighs and leans toward me. "Look, you know how I feel about you." He gestures with one hand. "I'm tired of hiding it from everyone. And I don't like having to sneak away for even a few minutes alone with you." He rubs my knuckles with his thumb.

I squeeze his hand lightly in return. "I know. Let's wait until we get back to D.C., and then we'll talk to Royal. Okay?" It's a stalling tactic. I'm still hoping I can convince Vale to keep it a secret.

Vale's eyes light up. "Really?"

"Really." I avert my eyes. I hate having to lie to him, but I've got to keep his head focused on the mission and not our relationship.

The coast is clear, so I scoot toward Vale. He leans in the rest of the way and gives me a soft kiss. I hear the chime that notifies the passengers that the lavatory is available and pull away from Vale, standing quickly.

He looks up at me still smiling.

Lotus walks toward us. "Dude. There's a shower in the bathroom!"

"No way." Vale shoots out of his seat and almost jogs up the aisle toward the lavatory.

I laugh, turning to Lotus. "Did you use it?"

Lotus reaches up to touch his afro. "A public shower? No way. There's no telling how well they actually clean that thing." He straightens his shoulders. "How do I look?"

I smile, glancing him over. His navy tee and black, relaxed fit jeans still look clean and unwrinkled. "Fine."

"Fine? That's all?" He cocks an eyebrow at me.

I shrug. "What are you going for?"

Lotus sighs and leans over to retrieve his black leather jacket, sliding into it like it's his second skin. "How about now?"

"Very cool." I scratch the back of my neck. "Isn't this line of questioning better suited for Clarity?"

Lotus laughs. "I'm going to go up front and ask if I can sit in the jump seat."

"Tell them it's your birthday."

He snorts and walks back up the aisle.

I head back to my seat and find Clarity eating a gargantuan chocolate chip cookie. "Want some?" She grins as she breaks off a piece of chewy goodness and holds it out to me.

"Yes, please." I lean back in my chair, savoring the melted chocolate and crumbly brown sugar taste in my mouth. "It's still warm," I say once I've swallowed.

"I think they heat them up in the microwave," Clarity says before taking another large bite.

"Whatever they're doing, it's working."

We eat in silence for a few minutes before I angle my body toward her. "Are you nervous about going back to Sicily?"

Clarity's chewing slows, and she adjusts in her seat. A weighty silence settles between us. Her eyes travel down to the floor and remain there as she ponders how to respond to the question. Finally, her eyes rise to meet mine. "Yes," she says, measuring her words. "I haven't been back there in sixteen years, but I want to know—"

I finish her sentence. "Where you came from."

Clarity nods. "It's my heritage."

"I totally understand that." I reach over and squeeze her forearm.

She gives me a faint smile. "I wish… I wish I had family there."

My heart breaks for her. Clarity's parents died in a devastating earthquake right before she turned two. It was a miracle she survived under the rubble; it was all that remained of her family home. Royal, who happened to be there on a mission, was helping with relief efforts when she was pulled from the dust and dirt. He made sure she got all the medical care she needed, and he used all of his vast array of resources to find other living family members, but there were none. So, he bundled up that tiny, olive-skinned, brown-eyed baby girl and brought her back to the states, to me.

"Don't ever forget that you are my family," I say, giving

her one more squeeze before retracting my hand. "Want another cookie?"

She nods, a pensive look on her face. "Yes, please."

I flag down a flight attendant and request two more of their delicious cookies, my mind whirring. We have way more resources now than my father did fifteen years ago. Maybe there's a way to figure out if Clarity has any living family, after we're done with our mission in London.

The flight attendant hands us our cookies and makes her way up the aisle.

My eyes turn to my sister as I bite into my cookie. If Clarity has any biological family left in Sicily, I'm going to find them.

Chapter 9

Once we reach Heathrow, the pilot expertly glides onto the runway and immediately I catch a glimpse of the nicely manicured patches of grass between the runways that crisscross the airport grounds. The landing is as smooth as the softened butter Vale uses for baking.

"Can you believe we're here?" Clarity beams at me as she cranes her neck to look out the window.

I shake my head. "Nope." I lean over to look past Clarity, but can't see much else. It's an unfortunate side effect of having cubbies in the middle row.

My watch vibrates.

Royal
Meet at baggage claim in 10.

Clarity and I gather our carry-ons and stand, waiting for our turn to exit the airplane. When we approach the door, she gives the pilot and flight attendant a relaxed smile. "That was amazing. Thank you."

The flight attendant who helped us to our seats at the beginning of the trip winks. "I'm glad you enjoyed your flight.

Have a wonderful time in London."

Clarity scrunches her shoulders up toward her ears and squeals. I don't think I've ever heard Clarity squeal before now. She's usually much more serene. But I get it. She's been dreaming of going back to Sicily since she was a little girl.

I, too, thank the flight crew before following Clarity out of the plane and into the terminal. I stop when I reach it, tilting my head back to look up at the great glass structure we are now standing in, and the cloudy sky beyond. It must be raining outside but I don't hear the telltale sound of rain striking glass.

Clarity grabs my hand. "Let's go."

We swing our hands as we walk through the airport toward the baggage claim area.

It feels eerie riding in a car on the left side of the road. I keep looking forward, expecting to be staring into the grill of an oncoming car. But as the ride continues, the bizarre feeling abates, leaving me more at ease. Our driver maneuvers the car expertly, and I watch his every move. I'll probably have to drive myself at some point during our trip, so it's smart to pay attention. Yet, my eyes keep gravitating toward the view outside my window instead.

London is gorgeous. I can't peel my eyes away from the windows as the open swaths of green around Heathrow give way to brick and masonry buildings as we near the heart of London. The massive stone arch that beckons onlookers toward the Victoria and Albert Museum causes a sharp intake of breath. It's captivating. And I thought some of the buildings in D.C. were beautiful. They are, don't get me wrong, but the buildings in London are much more regal. These ornate edifices hold hundreds of years of history. My heart pounds in my chest. I love London. I only just arrived and I never want to leave.

A gentle hand on my thigh jolts me back to reality. "Beautiful, isn't it?" Clarity whispers, her hushed tone reverent as she too strains to peer out the back windows of our luxury sedan. Apparently, Darnay tried to send a limousine for us, but Royal refused. I can imagine him now, saying limousines were "too flashy," and that we're supposed to "blend in, not stand out." He's right. Darnay seems pretty rusty at the rules of espionage.

"Yes." I nod in agreement, twisting in my seat to peer at the car behind us, in which Royal and the guys are riding, but I can't see them.

"We're almost to Darnay Plaza London. This is Grosvenor Square," intones the driver from up front.

I nod, taking in our surroundings. The square is lush and green, with tall trees whose branches reach outward in all directions, creating a canopy of shade around the edge of the park.

We pull up in front of a vast, four-story building. It's beautiful, red-brick facade has an ornate series of arches over each window. Spires along the roofline point upward to the gray sky. There's even a clock in the tallest tower. Intricately carved stone corbels unfurl above the oversized front entry. A black canopy with golden lettering spans the door, and a doorman in a full, dark green uniform with a black, gold-trimmed hat stands at the ready to receive us.

Clarity and I slide out of the car, our eyes gazing upward at the fancy hotel. The Darnay Plaza London.

The driver pops the trunk and unloads our luggage for us, setting it on the curb.

"Need help with that?" Vale asks, coming over.

I open my mouth to speak, but am interrupted by three

porters who are also in dark green uniforms with black hats trimmed in gold. "Welcome to the Darnay Plaza London," one of them says as they scoop up our bags.

"Thanks," I say, meeting Clarity's eyes. She scrunches her nose in excitement.

Royal puts one hand on my shoulder. "How was your drive?"

"Fantastic," Clarity sighs, smiling.

"I'm glad." He looks up at the hotel in front of us, and I take the opportunity to study him. Our long plane ride has left stark wrinkles in Royal's gray tweed suit and black knit turtleneck. His face is drawn and missing the color that usually saturates his tan skin. He must feel my eyes on him, because his gaze turns to me. "I'm fine," he says with a wan smile. "Travel simply wears on me more than it used to." His eyes move to Clarity, and a chuckle escapes his lips.

I can see why. She's almost bouncing up and down on the sidewalk, excitement radiating from her at the thought of being in such a wondrous place, and so far from home.

She turns to meet Royal's look, and a smile spreads across her lips. "I'm so glad we're here," she breathes. "This is going to be an amazing trip."

I clear my throat. "Don't forget, we have work to do." I nudge her side with my elbow.

"I won't." She shakes her head and turns back to the front of the hotel.

Royal studies her for a moment before locking eyes with me. "Let her be," he mouths.

I stand back on my heels. I need to relax and enjoy this trip. A glance down at my watch gives me the time and weather forecast for London over the next three days.

With expert precision, the porters pack our luggage onto

the shiny brass cart, their faces betraying nothing when they handle our weapons cases. Of course, they may not know what's in them, but the hard, black matte shells and combination locks on the handles make it pretty obvious that we don't want prying eyes.

"Welcome to the Darnay Plaza London," the doorman says, sweeping his arm to lead us into the hotel. We step into the revolving door one by one and enter the building.

"Oh crap," Lotus says when we step inside. He's not wrong.

The foyer of the hotel is smaller than I imagined, but breathtaking. Sunlight pours into the room through a large, round skylight of leaded glass in a sunburst pattern. Wrought iron sconces augment the natural light, putting off a soft, warm glow. The floor is covered in a check pattern of gray and white marble tiles, the variegation in the stone striking in its contrast. To our right, an arched staircase travels upward, its wrought iron railing trimmed by a shiny brass handrail.

A young woman, probably twenty-five, wearing a dark green skirt suit and killer black heels strides toward us, a wide smile on her face. Her box braids are pulled back from her face in a low ponytail. She grasps Royal's outstretched hand. "Y'all must be the private school group from the States? Welcome to our hotel. We're so glad to have you." Her Georgian accent is divine. She would make reading gun safety manuals riveting with that voice.

Using my well-practiced skills of observation, I look her over, and notice a small bulge at her side. She's got a handgun in a holster under her blouse. I move my hand slowly downward to rest at my waist, where my karambits are hidden beneath my wide belt.

"That's us," Royal says, shaking her hand, a warm smile on

his face. "Is Charles Darnay here?" He looks past the young woman down the hallway whence she came.

The woman's smile doesn't falter. "He's away at the moment, so I'll be helping you get settled in. I can show you to where you'll be working. If you'll follow me." I relax my fingers, but my hand doesn't leave my belt. She turns and walks down a hallway to the left of the check-in desk, which is a wide expanse of mahogany wood that gleams in the cool, white light filtering in from the skylight.

"You can call me Julep," she says over her shoulder as she walks past a room where a young security guard sits with his side to us in front of a bank of monitors, watching the feeds from the security cameras around the hotel. The guard sits upright in his chair, alert and ready. He nods at Julep as she passes.

I lower my hand from my belt, but remain at the ready. If it's one thing working in this business has taught me, it's not to trust anyone at first. Least of all pretty young women.

Julep leads us into a long, narrow conference room with a table that spans the length of it. There's a sumptuous spread of finger sandwiches, scones, petits fours, and fruit at the far end. A large, pure white teapot sits in the center of it all emitting steam from its spout.

Turning to Royal, she speaks. "You must be Royal. I've heard so much about you. Mr. Darnay can't seem to keep quiet about all of your adventures." Royal smiles broadly.

"I hope he hasn't told you too much. Most of our work is classified."

Julep smiles knowingly. "Don't worry about that. I have clearance."

At that, Royal laughs. "Excellent."

My eyebrows raise a bit before I can stop them. He isn't

normally so open and friendly with strangers. He's not unfriendly, exactly, but much more subdued. He's either attracted to Julep, or really excited to see Darnay again. Possibly both.

As if sensing my surprise, Julep catches my eye and winks.

Royal clears his throat. "Let me introduce you to the rest of my team." He turns to us. "This is Loveday, my oldest daughter. Clarity, my younger daughter, and this is Vale, and Lotus."

Julep smiles at each of us in turn. "It's a pleasure to meet you all. Please, get yourselves something to eat, and sit. Who wants tea?" She moves toward the spread and pours the walnut brown liquid into delicate tea cups, asking each of us how we take it. "Personally, I prefer it iced, but hot tea is traditional here."

"Same," Vale says. "Sweet tea is the best."

"It's nice to meet a fellow southerner," Julep says as she prepares his tea, handing it to him with a steady hand.

"When was the last time you were there?" Vale asks, taking a sip from the steaming cup. He's doing it again—asking questions to steer the conversation. He's good at drawing people out that way.

Once we're all seated, munching on snacks and sipping our tea, Julep formally begins our meeting. "Mr. Darnay is very appreciative that you have come. He wishes he could be here himself, but…" She gives a wave of her hand. "He had business at another of his properties."

"When will he be back?" Royal asks between bites of his chicken salad sandwich.

Julep wipes at the corners of her mouth with her white cloth napkin before responding. "I can't answer that, but I can tell you why Mr. Darnay asked you to come to London."

Royal nods. "Please do."

"Mr. Darnay hired me to be the head of security at his properties here in London, but I could use some help. There has been a string of car thefts from valets at several of the luxury hotels here in the city, and Mr. Darnay is worried that his hotels are next."

"Why not just beef up security in the parking lot?" I ask, sitting forward in my chair.

Julep nods. "He would, but the National Crime Agency has asked him to take it a step further. They want him to trace the cars to see if the thieves are acting as part of a larger car smuggling operation. They suspect that's the case, because a vast majority of the cars taken are luxury vehicles."

I furrow my eyebrows. "Can't they do that themselves?" I take a bite of a white chocolate petit four and it melts in my mouth.

Clarity sits beside me, watching me.

I point to what's left of the miniature cake in my hand and give a thumbs up.

She grins, picks up her own, and begins to nibble at it.

"They would, but Mr. Darnay has certain resources that the NCA simply doesn't have, due to his many years of service to the government." Julep sweeps her hand toward us. "That's where all of you come in. Mr. Darnay wants you to investigate the car thefts for him to figure out who is stealing the cars, who the thieves are working for, and where the cars are being taken."

Royal nods. "It sounds pretty straightforward."

Julep smiles. "I'm so glad you think so. Mr. Darnay would like you to begin surveilling the valet parking areas at three of his hotels here in the city this evening. Will that work for you?"

"That will be fine." He turns to us. "Loveday, what do you

say?"

I keep my face blank, serious, as I nod. "We can handle it, but we'll need our own vehicles."

"Mr. Darnay has seen to that. There are four BMW 7 Series Saloons in the parking garage below the hotel, and one Suzuki Hayabusa."

"I call the motorcycle," Lotus jumps in, rubbing his hands together. "I've always wanted to get my hands on one of those Suzukis."

Julep's eyes sparkle. "Royal told us that you'd prefer it to a car."

"He was right." He turns to Royal. "Thanks, man."

"You're welcome," Royal says with a chuckle.

"I want a shot at that thing too," Vale says. He and Lotus fist bump across the table.

"If that's everything," Julep says with a satisfied smile, "I'll show you to your rooms so you can get some rest before tonight. I'll have all of your surveillance equipment ready this evening."

Clarity speaks up. "I'd like to room with Loveday, if that's all right."

I give her a small smile before catching Vale's eye. He shakes his head slightly. I guess we won't be getting any alone time after all, unless I can sneak past Clarity. And that's doubtful.

"That'll be just fine," Julep says as she leads us back up the hall toward the opulent hotel lobby. Sunlight catches the crystals in the chandelier and casts prisms that dance over the room.

Chapter 10

"Where do you suggest we eat dinner?" Royal asks Julep as she climbs the stairs to the second floor.

"Our restaurant here at the hotel is excellent. It's got three Michelin stars."

"Sounds great."

"I'll meet you at the conference room at 21:00 with the details of the hotels you'll be watching this evening. Then we'll eat a quick dinner."

Julep leads us into the elevator and takes us up to the fourth story, the top floor of the hotel.

Clarity's and my hotel room is gorgeous. The entire room is blanketed with white, and there is wallpaper on the wall behind the bed that displays a forest of white birch trees, stark and leafless in winter. There are two king-size beds, each surrounded by a gauzy canopy that opens and closes with the flick of the wrist. The carpet is a diamond pattern of velvety, pearly gray that feels like soft sand between my toes.

Clarity sighs when she sees it and swan dives onto her bed.

"I have to admit, this definitely beats the Tower." I set my bag down on a luggage rack and unlock it, shrugging out of my trench coat and draping it over the open case. Then, I kick off my shoes and stretch my toes as wide as I can. The pulling sensation in the pads of my feet feels amazing.

"I don't think I can sleep. I'm too excited." Clarity sits cross-legged in the middle of her bed with her chin propped in her hands and eyes dreamy.

"I know, but it sounds like it's going to be a long night."

Clarity nods. "You're right." She crawls off her bed and shimmies out of her slacks, leaving them in a puddle on the floor. "Let's try to get some rest." She climbs into her bed and we both tuck ourselves in. I flick the light switch on the nightstand and our room settles into darkness.

My watch vibrates, and I sit straight up in bed, wide awake. Looking over at Clarity's bed, all I see is a lump under the covers. She is still fast asleep. I push out from under the thick, velvet blankets and scoot off the bed, padding across the carpet to where she is snoozing. I ease a pillow off her bed, raise it up above my head, and bring it down hard on the lump that is my sister's sleeping form.

"What are you doing?"

I whirl around to see Clarity standing in the bathroom doorway, toothbrush in hand. She laughs. "Thought you'd catch me by surprise?"

I smile wide. "I guess not."

"Maybe next time." Clarity returns to the bathroom and starts brushing her teeth.

I walk over to my gun case and use the combination on the hand scanner. I place my palm on the surface and the screen beeps almost immediately, unlocking the case. "Which gun are you taking tonight?"

"Probably my Smith & Wesson." Clarity walks over and stands beside me, looking down at my collection of weaponry.

"And you? Glock 19?"

I nod. It's my weapon of choice, besides my karambits. I'd rather disable an opponent, but I'll shoot them if I have to. At least that's what I've been trained to do. I've never actually had to shoot someone before, except with tranquilizer darts.

We meet up in the conference room right at 21:00. The table is covered with tiny, high-tech cameras and listening equipment. There's a computer set up, connected to four screens, all blank. A large drone sits at one end, its black arms reaching outward in six different directions. Royal and the guys are standing over the flying machine, pointing at it.

Lotus rubs his hands. "Can I fly it?"

"I think I'll leave the flying to Julep and myself," Royal says, giving Lotus a pat on the back.

"Aww man."

I take a step closer to check out the drone for myself, but Julep speaks, halting my progress. It's time to focus on our instructions and not on the top-of-the-line, flying surveillance drone, even though it's a mere few feet away from me, and it looks awesome.

"Have a seat everyone." She stands at the front of the room, waiting until we're all seated around the table to continue. "As I mentioned this afternoon, Mr. Darnay would like your team to watch three of his hotels here in the city. Is that a problem?"

"Loveday, Lotus, and Clarity can handle it," Royal says.

"I thought so."

"Royal?" Vale speaks, stepping toward the table. "I'd like to be sent into the field too. Maybe Loveday could show me the ropes?"

Royal opens his mouth to speak, but I beat him to it. "No.

You're more help to us here at the comms, keeping us apprised of each other's movements."

Vale frowns. "I think I can be a valuable asset in the field, and if we're just watching cars—"

"Loveday is right," Royal says, backing me up. "We need you here, keeping everyone in touch. We can talk about you going into the field another time."

Vale shoves his hands into the pockets of his black athletic pants, frustration simmering behind his eyes. He gives a curt nod. "Yes, sir," he says, pointedly avoiding looking at me.

My face remains blank. I'd rather him assume I don't think he's ready than let him know the truth: that I can't risk him being in the field because the idea of him getting hurt terrifies me. I have to keep him safe. Besides, Lotus and Clarity are simply more prepared for field-work than Vale. He's been working hard on his marksmanship and stealth, but he's still better at languages and logistics than getting the drop on any of us during training. He's the first one caught in our capture the flag games every time. Vale is almost ready, but he needs more practice before he starts field-work.

An hour later I'm sitting in my BMW Saloon in the parking garage underneath another of Darnay's hotels, on the north side of London. Clarity is to the east, and Lotus is stationed at Darnay Plaza.

Vale has been uncharacteristically silent on the comms. He's definitely miffed at me now.

I reach up to make sure my earbud is on. "How is it looking, Clarity?" I ask, wading into the silence of our open communication channel.

"All clear here. We've had a couple of patrons who lost their tickets, but the valet remembered them."

"They shouldn't be handing out car keys without a ticket," Vale says in a tone of frustration.

"Easy pickings," Lotus says. I can tell by his voice that he's grinning.

"You would think that," I say, smirking. "Was that your scheme, before?"

Lotus laughs in response. "A car thief never tells."

"But these people genuinely lost their ticket," Clarity, always the optimist. "It happens."

"There's got to be a way to close that loophole." I shift in my seat, my eyes never leaving the entrance to the valet lot here at the Luxury London.

"I think I've got something," Lotus says, his voice coming through my earbud. "There's a tweenager strolling through the parking lot, scanning cars."

"A tweenager?" Clarity sounds incredulous.

"They start them young," Lotus says.

"Keep eyes on him," I say. "You could be right."

There's silence over the line for a minute, and then, "Oh hell no. I'm going over there." There's a creak as Lotus dismounts his motorcycle, and then the sound of his feet pounding on pavement. "What are you doing?" His voice is loud but controlled.

"Nothing." It's a surly response, but the speaker sounds young, even to me.

"Nothing my ass," Lotus says. "Then why do you have a coat hanger in your pants?"

I hear a grunt and then feet running away across the pavement.

"Lotus, status update?" It's the first thing Vale has said in a few minutes.

"I'm fine," Lotus says. "The kid shoved me, and then he

ran off. I don't think he's a member of the crew we're looking for. He was a total amateur."

"Head back to your vehicle." Vale's words are short, clipped.

"Will do." I hear his footsteps across the parking lot. "This bike is sweet." In his enthusiasm, he draws out the last word. "Maybe they'll let me take it back to D.C."

"We'll see." I'm doubtful. It would be a pretty expensive gift.

Royal doesn't shoot down Lotus's hope, which surprises me. I put a piece of peppermint gum into my mouth and start chewing. My jaw pops.

"What are you eating?" Clarity asks.

"I'll give you one guess."

"Gum," she and I say at the same time.

She crunches into what sounds like an apple.

"I'm hungry too," Lotus says. "How come you didn't pack me any snacks?"

"You're a big boy," I say. "You should have gotten your own."

Ordinarily, a line like that would have drawn at least a chuckle from Vale, but tonight it doesn't. Instead, the line goes silent again.

Chapter 11

My diaphragm expands as I take in a breath and hold it, listening. Clarity sounds like she's asleep, finally. Her excitement about being in London kept her up forever.

I peel myself out of bed and stand, squinting through the dark toward my sister's bed. The darkness in the room curls around her bed, masking any movement, so I tiptoe toward the door. It's a good thing I sleep in a black tank and knit pants, because if she is awake it'll be harder for her to see me. I unlock the door and open it slowly. It emits a loud squeak, and I freeze in the doorframe, waiting to see if it's woken Clarity. She doesn't stir.

Mercifully, the door shuts soundlessly, freeing me to go down the hall to Vale's room. I tap on the door to Vale's hotel room. "Are you in there?" It's a whisper, as I'm trying to keep from waking the other guests. It is 03:00 after all. We finally came back to the Darnay Plaza around 02:00. There hadn't been any movement after Lotus scared off that kid, so Julep gave the all clear.

Vale hasn't said more than two words to me since our meeting this evening. We need to clear the air. I tap on the door again, but there's no response. He's not a heavy sleeper, so he's either ignoring my knock or he's not in his room. I start next door to ask Lotus if Vale is with him, but an idea jerks my head up. There's somewhere else Vale might be right now. I scan the hallway, then jog to the end where there's a discrete list of hotel amenities mounted by the elevators. The indoor pool is on the roof.

I take the elevator up to the top and step out into the lowly lit room. The entire space is enclosed in glass, and most of the lights are out, showcasing a view of the city spread out before us. I scan the room. There isn't anyone on the deck, but there is a pile of dry clothing and a towel on one of the lounge chairs. The cast from the water leaves blue shimmers on the glass as I step toward the pool.

Vale is there, gliding silently under the water in his swim trunks and goggles.

After rolling up the legs of my pants, I sit on the edge and dip my feet into the water. It's warm, and it feels good on my skin. I splash around to let Vale know that I'm here.

He swims across the pool and surfaces a few feet from me, holding onto the concrete edge with one hand. Our eyes meet, but he doesn't say anything for a beat. Finally, he speaks. "Why did you stop me from going in the field?"

I study his face, his square jaw is clenched, and his green eyes are locked on to me, piercing through my armor, but I don't look away. I could try lying, but what would be the point? "I need to keep you safe."

He's still as the water ripples around his shoulders. "Is that it? Or is it that you don't think I'm good enough?"

I consider this before answering. "Both." The truth again.

He huffs in frustration. "I need you to trust me."

I relax my legs, allowing their buoyancy to pull them to the surface. "I do trust you. It's everyone else I don't trust."

His lips are flat as he swims toward me. He slides a hand up my calf and lets it rest behind the crook of my knee. "Hey." He gives me a small smile. "I can do this. You have to let me try."

I study him before responding. "Are you asking as my teammate or as my boyfriend?"

He smiles now, biting his bottom lip. "Would it make a difference?"

One corner of my mouth curls upward. "Maybe." I pull my tank top off over my head and toss it away toward one of the lounge chairs, followed by my knit pants.

Vale watches my every move as I slide into the water beside him, wearing only my black boyshort-cut underwear and a sports bra.

"Race you." I dive under the water and make for the opposite end of the pool.

I'm sitting in my parked BMW at the back of the valet lot, at the same hotel as the night before. Clarity and Lotus have resumed their positions as well. Tonight, Vale is with Clarity. It's the result of a short conversation Royal had with me, in which he shared his opinion that it's as good a time as any to put Vale in the field, given the low risk of our assignment. I disagreed with him, of course, but my flimsy reasons for holding Vale back were met with nothing more than an expressionless stare. Once it was decided, I was sorely tempted to bring Vale with me, but it's not like we can make out when we're on a job. Plus, Clarity could teach Vale a few things about sneaking around, so my boyfriend is with my sister and Royal is at the Plaza, running the comms.

A guy wearing jeans and a nondescript T-shirt exits the hotel and moves toward the valet parking area. He glances to both sides before approaching the valet, his hands fidgeting back and forth from his pockets to his sides.

"I think I've got something." My eyes narrow as I watch him talking to the valet.

The valet, a young guy probably about my age, shakes his head.

The guy makes a show of going through his pockets, and then holds his hands up toward the parking attendant, apparently pleading.

After a second, the valet nods and retrieves the keys from the board behind him.

The guy smiles apologetically as he takes the keys. Then he strolls across the lot and runs a hand over the hood of a pristine white Lexus. "I may have something. Royal, can you check surveillance at my location for the last minute and compare gray T-shirt guy to the person who dropped off a white Lexus with the license plate number Lima Alpha One Eight Papa Delta Quebec?"

The sound of a car peeling out screeches through my earbud.

"What was that?" Clarity asks.

"Someone snuck past me," Lotus says. A muffled curse reaches me. "I'm going after him."

"Remember, follow him. Don't try to catch him. We want to see where he goes." Royal's voice is calm, steady.

"Got it." Lotus's motorcycle rumbles to life.

The guy I've been watching unlocks the Lexus and slides inside. He rubs his hands together, and then backs out of his parking space.

"You were right, Loveday. He's not the owner. Follow him."

"Got it." A wave of adrenaline courses through me. Here

we go. I start my car and ease out of the lot after the white car. It's nearly 01:00, but traffic is still fairly heavy. I keep two cars between my BMW and the Lexus I'm following, just in case the driver is as shifty as he looks.

"Lotus? Status?" Royal asks, and waits for a response.

"I'm in pursuit," Lotus says loudly over the thrumming of his bike.

"Clarity?"

"We may have something. Can you check surveillance on a car with the license plate number Lima Alpha One Eight Kilo Charlie Romeo? We've got a young woman unlocking the car."

"Give me a second."

The line is silent but for Royal's typing. "It's her car," he says finally. "Stay where you are. Lotus?"

"We're heading east toward one of the docks along the river. He hasn't seen me."

"Keep it that way."

"Roger that."

I snicker. "You've been watching too many James Bond movies."

"Whatever," Lotus says. "Over and out."

"Do not under any circumstances remove your earbud," Royal says sternly.

"Geez. It was a joke."

I smirk into the darkness. This is so much more fun than when it was just Royal, Clarity, and me.

Up ahead, the car I'm tailing breaks out of the traffic and speeds ahead. A wall of cars closes in around me. "Crap. I'm losing him."

I attempt to maneuver my car through the traffic, but I'm not fast enough.

The Lexus takes a right turn out of sight.

I honk in an attempt to get people to move, but the cars aren't budging. The light turns red. I let out a grunt, frustrated. "He's gone. Royal, do you have him on traffic cameras?"

"Give me a minute."

"What was the license plate?" Lotus asks. "I might have him. A white Lexus just passed me."

"Lima Alpha One Eight Papa Delta Quebec," I chime in.

"I've got him. He and my guy are driving into the shipyard. Should I follow?"

"Park your motorcycle and follow on foot," Royal says, voice tranquil. "Do not engage."

"Yes, sir." The sound of the motorcycle cuts off. It's quiet for a moment, then Lotus whispers. "There's a security booth at the gate, but the guard isn't there. I'm going in now."

"Find a place to observe, and wait for Loveday to meet you. Loveday?"

I finally break through the traffic and take a deep breath to slow my heart rate. "Send me the address. I'm on my way." It takes a few minutes, but I get out of the bottleneck and drive through London, following the BMW's GPS system. "I'll be there in five."

"There's no rush. They're loading the cars into shipping containers. There's a cargo ship docked in the river. My guess is they're going to load the cars onto that. If I could get closer, I might be able to figure out where they're shipping them."

"Wait for Loveday."

I follow the GPS down a long street and around the corner. Ahead of me, I can see the orange glow of lights in the shipyard. "I'm right outside." I catch sight of Lotus's motorcycle parked on the street, and pull in a few spaces down. It's cold, and I wish I'd worn a couple more layers, but If I end up climbing the bright yellow crane that's standing in the middle of the yard, I'll be glad I'm not wearing my trench coat. I approach the gate to the shipyard, my movements casual as I eye the security booth. The guard is walking toward it, sipping on a steaming cup of coffee. I crouch down as I skirt past the booth and through the gate, ducking behind a shipping container. "Lotus, where are you?" I whisper.

"I'm on top of a blue shipping container to the north of the crane."

I peek out from behind the container, my fingers cold against the metal, and scan the yard. There are stacks of shipping containers on either side of the crane. A mobile office building sits to one side, its windows dark. There's movement on top of one of the shipping containers. Lotus. "I can see your feet. Slide toward the middle of the container."

Lotus's feet disappear.

I take a deep breath and take another look around the yard. There are lights on stands around one of the shipping containers. A man comes out and moves to one side, lighting a cigarette. T-shirt man joins the smoker outside the container, his arms crossed, looking toward the entrance. They're waiting for something.

"I've got two guys outside a lit container at your 3. See anyone else?"

"No," Lotus says. "Just those two. The cars are in the container."

"I'm heading your way." I take a deep breath and run toward the middle of the shipyard, where Lotus is hiding, careful to stay out of sight.

"We've got one," Clarity says, her voice smooth as glass. "Red Mercedes Benz." She gives the specs on the driver.

"Not the owner," Royal says. "Follow them. And be careful."

"Yes, Dad."

I smile. Even in the midst of a mission, Clarity calls him dad. I almost never call him that, and definitely not when I'm working. It's easier for me to compartmentalize if I call him by his code name instead. It keeps me focused.

"Loveday? Where are you?" Lotus asks.

"Just a second." I weave between shipping containers, pausing whenever I have to cross an open space. Luckily, the hulking metal boxes are placed around the lot at random, and their shadows loom large under the overhead lights that line the yard. I reach Lotus's container and scramble up the end of it, using the hinges to pull myself up over the edge. It's a good thing I've done a fair amount of urban climbing.

Lotus lifts his chin in greeting.

I slither toward him and we lay there, side by side on our stomachs, watching the guys to our right.

Cigarette guy has started a second smoke, and T-shirt guy is still standing there, waiting.

"I wonder what they're waiting for? Clarity?" I whisper.

"We're still following the red Mercedes, but we're heading your way. Be there in four minutes." A horn sounds through my earbud.

I meet Lotus's eyes. "We'll maintain position." My handgun digs into my side where it's tucked into its holster under my shirt, but I don't dare move. I shiver against the cold metal container, wishing again that I'd worn more than a single long-sleeved shirt.

Lotus scoots next to me, pressing his leg against mine. "Better?" he mouths.

I nod and give him a small smile.

"Clarity, when you arrive, take up position outside the gate and wait for Lotus and Loveday. Vale will follow your lead."

More typing.

"Yes, Dad."

The minutes drag out as we wait. I can taste the salt in the wet ocean air as it settles down around us.

"The car is pulling up to the security booth," Clarity says. "We're parking across the street."

"Good," Royal says. "I've got the drone over the yard. Loveday, can you get into the office? We need to get a look at the shipping manifest."

I scan the yard. "I don't see anyone else. I can make it." I turn to Lotus. "Cover me."

Just as I'm about to jump down to the ground, car headlights stream across the asphalt below me. I freeze where I'm crouched at the edge of the container as the red Mercedes drives past toward the open container.

I turn to Lotus, who is staring at me, eyes wide. "That was close," he breathes.

The car pulls into the container and stops. The driver shuts off the car and gets out, barely squeezing between the car's side panel and the inside wall of the container. "Is that it?" he asks Cigarette man.

I wait until he's talking, and then I use the noise to cover the sound of my feet landing on the pavement. I look back up at Lotus, who gestures for me to advance toward the office. He's crouched at the edge of the container now, holding his handgun at the ready.

"Four tonight." The man grins in response. "Not bad." All three of them enter the container.

"They're using straps to raise the Mercedes up over the Lexus," Lotus says. "I bet they could fit another car in there."

I'm slinking around the shipping container when Royal speaks through the comms.

"We've got a problem."

I freeze, standing in shadow, my back pressed up against the corrugated metal. "What?" I whisper.

There's a tinge of annoyance in Royal's voice as he responds. "The Lexus was Charles Darnay's car. There's a thumb drive hidden in it, under the drive stick boot, and he needs it back. Can you get to it?"

I glance up at Lotus, who looks toward the container. "They're still inside, securing the car. You'll have to wait until they're done."

My heart is pounding. The longer I stand here the more likely it is that I'll be caught. I steal around to the far side, away from the office.

"They're coming out of the container," Lotus whispers.

Their voices carry toward me, though I can't hear what they're saying.

"They're moving toward the office. One of them said that's the last car."

I wait, ready to fly at the sight of opposition.

"They're going inside. The door is closed. Now's your chance. Go."

I sprint across the yard toward the lit container, sliding inside. There's plenty of space between the Mercedes and the wall for me to slide past. I ease through to where Darnay's Lexus is parked. "I'm in. Where's the thumb drive?"

"It's under the leather around the shifter," Royal says, then he changes tacks. "Clarity, enter the yard and take up a position on the roof of the office. As soon as they leave, get inside and see if you can find the shipping manifest."

"Yes, Dad."

"And me?" Vale asks.

"Remain at the gate."

The line goes silent.

My pulse quickens as I eye the lack of space around the Lexus. "Guys, I don't know if I can get into the car." My eyes study the available space. There's no way I can get in through any of the car's doors, but there is a three foot gap between the vehicle's roof and the ceiling of the shipping container. "Wait. I think I have a way in." I hop onto the hood of the car and climb onto the roof. I curse under my breath. The sunroof is shut tight.

"Loveday?" Royal asks.

"Give me a second." I take my laser glass cutter out of my belt and start etching the glass in a wide circle, big enough that I can fit through.

"We've got company," Lotus says, his voice sounding stressed. "They're coming out of the office."

"How much time do I have?" I ask, still working the glass cutter.

"Maybe a minute."

I close the circle I've etched in the glass, shove the cutter back in my utility belt, and swivel around so my feet are above the glass. I stomp down once, twice, and the glass gives way.

"Loveday, get out of there." Lotus's voice is urgent.

I'm on my stomach now, lowering myself into the cabin of the car. "I'm almost there."

"There's not enough time. Get out of there. Now!" He's speaking louder now.

If he doesn't quiet down, they'll hear him.

"Loveday!" Royal barks.

"Coming." I curse as I slide off the car and shove through the narrow space between it and the wall. My heart is pounding as I reach the door of the container.

"Run!" Lotus yells, his worried voice carrying across the

yard.

But before I have the chance, I hear the sounds of footsteps right outside the container.

I'm trapped.

Chapter 12

From just outside, a man yells, "Someone's here!"

I screw up my courage and explode out of the container, ready for a fight. I almost run smack into Cigarette man. His cronies are just behind him. A quick scan tells me that he's the only one armed with a pistol at his waist. I pivot to the side and slam my forearm into his trachea. His hands fly up to his throat as he gasps for air.

His friends glare at me, but I've got my handgun out before they can react, my body squared to the side. "Don't move," I intone, holding my weapon steady. "Raise your hands."

Their eyes shift over my shoulder and I can feel Lotus standing behind me.

"Shit," T-shirt guy says. "Fine." Two of them comply, holding their arms in the air above their heads. Cigarette man is still gasping for air, clutching his throat.

I back away from them toward the shipping container without lowering my gun.

"I'm inside," Clarity whispers through the comm. "There's a ledger on the desk."

"Take photos," Royal says. It's reassuring to know he's

watching us via drone, waiting to see what's going to happen.

I feel the shipping container at my back and edge my way around its side.

Lotus is behind me, completely shielded by the container. "On my go," I whisper, "run. We'll take your motorcycle."

"Got it."

My eyes never leave the three men. They're all glaring at us, hands still aloft.

"Now," I say, and Lotus and I sprint across the yard, jumping over the security gate and darting toward the Suzuki parked at the curb.

"Hey!" The security guard yells as he fumbles to a stand, overturning his coffee on his desk.

A figure moves outside the fence. It's Vale, standing in the shadows, holding his tranquilizer gun at the ready. He ducks around the gate, darting the security guard in the neck.

"Nice shot," I say, but I can't stop. Lotus and I are on the motorcycle in a second and Lotus speeds away.

The crack of a bullet being fired reaches my ears as we speed around the corner.

"Clarity, are you out?" I ask, panting. "Vale?"

"We're out," she says. "Easy peasy."

She's done it again. My sister is as silent as a cat, and moves like one too, all taut stealth.

"We're ducking down in the car now. As soon as the car thieves go back inside the gate, we'll be on our way."

"Excellent," I say as I tighten my grip around Lotus's midsection. "Park around the block. I'll sneak back for the car." I yell in his ear.

"Roger that," he whoops as we careen down the street and take a corner at full speed.

Clarity's voice comes over my earbud just as Lotus is

cutting the engine on his bike. "We've got another problem."

"What is it?" I ask, moving over the sidewalk toward my car, being careful to stay below the sight line of anyone in the shipyard.

"They're preparing to load the shipping container with Darnay's car onto the freighter."

Vale chimes in. "I'm looking at the manifest, and if I'm reading it correctly, they're leaving for Port Klang in an hour."

My stomach drops. "I shouldn't have left that container without the drive."

"You would have been trapped," Lotus says at my shoulder.

"You and Clarity could have gotten me out," I say. It's true. I trust them both with my life.

"And me," Vale says. "I'd have helped."

I don't respond. Now isn't the time for that argument.

Royal breaks the tension. "Clarity, can you get into the container and retrieve the thumb drive?"

She hesitates before saying, "Yes."

I shake my head in the dark, but hold my tongue.

"Do it," Royal says.

Did he not hear the flicker in her voice? I stand up and peer over a car into the yard. The security guard is asleep in his chair in the booth, the tranquilizer dart removed. There's another man standing beside the snoozing guard, handgun in hand. We can't get back in that way.

I scan the fence. It's eight feet tall and rimmed with coils of barbed wire. I turn toward Lotus, who is crouched beside me, behind a car. "Got any bolt cutters?"

"Sure, let me get them out of my pocket," he says, rolling his eyes.

I exhale through my nose, frustrated.

"Clarity? Are you okay?"

When she finally speaks, her voice is quiet, sad. I strain to focus on her words. "I can't get inside the crate," she says. "They're loading it with the crane. I'm sorry."

"It's fine," Royal says, his voice the essence of calm.

"We'll get onto the ship," I say, relieved that Clarity isn't sneaking into the shipping container. "No problem."

Clarity speaks, her voice more confident this time. "We'll meet you at the south side of the yard. There's a stack of containers three high that they're not loading."

I take a long look at the fence again. There's no way we're getting inside. The security guard is still asleep, but there are two other men with him now, both armed. They've sure beefed up security in the last several minutes. Beyond the security booth, the shipping yard is crawling with men working, preparing the freighter for launch.

Lotus lets out a low whistle.

"Clarity, are you and Vale safe?" I ask.

My watch buzzes. It's a single word text message from Vale: *Yes*. Wherever they are, they can't risk speaking.

"Stay where you are until things quiet down. And stay out of sight."

Another message: a *thumbs up* emoji.

Lotus and I retreat down the sidewalk and slide into my BMW. We hunker down in the dark to wait.

Finally, all of the workers drain out of the yard, moving either onto the freighter or off down the street to other docks. But I already know that getting onto the freighter will be tricky, if not impossible.

"Loveday, status?" Royal asks.

I speak without lowering the binoculars from my eyes. "There are ten armed guards all along the deck of the freighter.

93

Even if we could tranq them all and get on board, we'd have to climb the stack to the shipping container, pick the lock, and then retrieve the thumb drive, all in about ten minutes. That's not counting getting back off the freighter. If we had more time, maybe…" I trail off as the freighter eases away from the dock. "Never mind. They're leaving."

Royal grunts in frustration. "Everyone report back to the Plaza, immediately."

Chapter 13

It's obvious now that our job is much bigger than tracking a ring of car thieves. Instead of simply turning in our findings and the ship's manifest to MI6, they've tasked us with recovering Darnay's thumb drive. Excuse me while I roll my eyes back into my head at him for leaving the stupid thing in his car. In a parking lot. When there were car thieves on a spree through London.

"Loveday." Royal's stern voice interrupts my mental ranting.

I sit up in my chair and make eye contact with him down the table. "Yes?"

He cocks an eyebrow at me before continuing. "I've run the face of every person who got on that freighter through the government's facial recognition software and none of them are anything more than petty criminals and car thieves. Several have assault charges to their name, but a couple of them don't even have criminal records." He's sitting at the head of the table, his laptop open in front of him. We're seated around the table, facing him.

Julep stands at his side, saying nothing. She prefers to stand 100% of the time, I've noticed. Seriously, the woman never sits down.

"So," I draw it out, thinking. "We gear up and hit them while they're on the open ocean, before they reach Port Klang." I lean forward, clasping my hands on the surface of the table.

Royal frowns. "No, doing something like that would draw too much attention from the media." He shakes his head as he speaks, looking at me from over his laptop.

"I can see the headline now," Lotus adds, grinning. "Pirates upgrade from ship to helicopter."

"Yes," Vale adds. "I'm Team Helicopter."

"Guys," Clarity says, face stern.

"Sorry," Lotus says, then mutters, "but it would be awesome."

Julep puts on an amused smile. "I've spoken to Mr. Darnay, and he agrees that we should travel to Malaysia and wait for the ship to arrive in a little over two weeks. Once the shipping containers are offloaded, we can get the car back and retrieve the thumb drive."

My eyebrows rise and my eyes widen. "That must be some important thumb drive." I adjust in my seat, leaning on the armrest with my left elbow. "What's on it?"

Julep gives me an appraising look. "It contains some sensitive information that Mr. Darnay would like returned." Her pointed expression is enough to stop my questions.

"Yes, ma'am."

A smile spreads across Lotus's face. "Wait, are you telling us we're going to Malaysia?"

Royal nods, steepling his fingers.

Julep cracks a smile. "That's exactly what we're telling you."

"Yes!" Lotus jumps out of his seat and claps. "This is

going to be awesome."

Vale pumps his fist. "Definitely."

"Our flight leaves in two days. I wanted to leave right away, but…" Royal stops speaking and looks up at Julep, whose eyes twinkle. "I convinced him to let you stay here for a couple of days, and really see London. You're going to love it."

"That's amazing," I say. I've always wanted to explore the city, visit the Tower of London, check out the security there, and plan a fake mission wherein I'm tasked with borrowing the crown jewels. I'd also like to try cockles, tiny clams found in London's East End. They're one of the few types of seafood I haven't tried. And riding the London Eye is definitely on my bucket list.

Clarity casts a furtive look at Royal, then catches my eye. She bobs her head slightly toward him.

I study her, and it dawns on me. "I'll ask him," I mouth. Maybe I won't be exploring London after all.

A smile fixes itself on Clarity's face. "He'll say yes if you ask him," she mouths back.

Royal casts his eyes down to his watch. "Our morning starts at 08:00 with a full English breakfast in the hotel restaurant, so get some sleep, everyone."

Lotus jumps up and gives Royal a fist bump before leaving the room, which makes him smile.

Vale follows him, stopping to thank Julep before moving off down the hall.

Clarity stands and gives Royal a big hug. "Night, Dad." She glances back at me before prancing away.

Julep is the last to leave. "Good night, Royal, Loveday." She smiles at me as she swishes past, her box braids grazing her shoulder blades. The only sound she makes as she retreats down the hall toward the hotel's opulent foyer is the muffled tap of her heels on the carpeted floor.

"Dad?" I go for the personal touch, hoping it'll soften him up before I make my request.

His blue eyes are piercing. "What is it, Loveday?" He can always read me, even when no one else can. Not even Clarity. I have more to learn about keeping my thoughts cloaked.

"I was thinking, if the ship with the stolen vehicles isn't scheduled to reach Port Klang for two weeks, we've got plenty of time to prepare to intercept them."

"Yes." He remains where he is, leaning forward, his forearms resting on the table.

"I'd like your permission to take Clarity to Sicily to look for her family."

He sits back, surprised. "I thought you were excited about seeing London?"

"I am, but Clarity's search for her family is more important. I can see London any time." My eyes drop to the table, then back up to meet his. It's true; I can see London another time. I don't know when I will, exactly, but I'm sure there will be time. Every day Clarity spends without her birth family is a day she can't get back.

Royal studies me without moving or saying anything. His eyes narrow slightly, the wheels in his head turning. Finally, he speaks. "I had hoped to take her myself."

"I know, but wouldn't it be better if you took the guys to Malaysia? That's our mission. The visit to Sicily is just a side task." I slide my hands in my trench coat pockets. I want to make it sound like Clarity and me traveling to another country on our own is no big deal, but I don't know if he'll buy me downplaying this. He knows what a huge step it would be, and how important visiting Sicily is to Clarity.

Royal purses his lips. "You're right. You and your sister

can certainly handle yourselves over there. But I want you to stick around here for a day or two, see the sights." He nods. "I'll make travel arrangements."

I grin. London and Sicily in one trip. This is excellent. "Thanks, Dad. Clarity will be thrilled."

He gives a small smile. "I know she will."

I turn to go, but stop in my tracks. "Do you have a copy of her birth certificate? That will give us a place to start."

He frowns. "I don't. They didn't have much information about Clarity when I adopted her. They were still scrambling after the earthquake, and I think they were just happy to have one more child taken care of."

It's my turn to nod. "I guess we'll start by looking for it, then. They must have a copy somewhere in their records."

My dad leans back in his chair and crosses one leg over the other. "I'm sure they do."

Chapter 14

There are a lot of things I could say about London, but their breakfasts are legit. My eyes about pop out of my head when the server at the hotel restaurant sets my breakfast plate in front of me. It's piled high with sausage, bacon, fried potatoes, sautéed mushrooms, beans, scrambled eggs, a slice of golden-brown buttered toast, and two dark slices of something I suspect to be black pudding. I catch Julep's eye down the table and point.

She rises out of her chair to see my plate. "It's black pudding, a type of blood sausage."

"Yeah, no," Lotus says, spearing his black pudding and setting it onto Clarity's plate. "You lost me at blood."

Clarity laughs, shaking her head. "Thanks?" She spears it on her fork, reaches across the table, and dumps it on Vale's plate.

Vale looks over at her with a disgusted expression, but doesn't move to retaliate.

I angle my face toward him. "Well?"

His eyes go wide as he looks at me. "What, you want me to try it right now?"

"Oh yeah."

He swallows, eyeing the black puddings. "Okay." He cuts a small piece and picks it up with his fork, bringing it to his nose. He sniffs it before popping it into his mouth, chewing slowly at first, then more quickly. "It's not bad," he says once he's swallowed it.

Lotus snorts in derision.

"Really," Vale says, taking another bite.

"Okay," Lotus says, "I'll play." He leans forward to take a piece off Vale's plate and takes a big bite, chewing cautiously.

"Well?" Julep asks from her spot at the end of the table, kitty corner to Lotus.

"It tastes kind of like oatmeal?" Lotus says at last. "Not what I thought."

"Want some more?" Julep asks, raising her hand to signal the waiter.

"No!" Lotus blurts, and we all bust up laughing. "No, thanks," he mumbles, eyeing the rest of his food.

Royal tries to suppress his deep, hearty laugh enough to speak to Julep. "I promise, they usually have better table manners."

Julep grins. "Don't worry about it. It's great being around other people closer to my age for a change."

"How old are you anyway?" Lotus asks.

Clarity shoots him a dirty look.

"What?" he asks, throwing up his hands. "She doesn't look that much older than us."

"It's okay," Julep says, "and you're right. You're what, nineteen?"

Lotus nods.

"I'm twenty-three."

"You're only four years older than me," Lotus says.

"And tMr. Darnay's head of security," Vale adds. "Wow."

"In some ways, age is just a number," Julep says. "Now let's eat."

We all tuck in, but I can't stop thinking about Julep's position here at Darnay Plaza London, despite her young age. It makes me feel better about being a spy at seventeen, like being in my line of work puts me in the company of a bunch of other kick-ass women, even if I don't know them. The few people I've met from Royal's time in the service were older guys, not unlike himself. I always figured they tended to travel in packs.

I glance up at Julep, who appears to be a young, attractive business woman, but my instincts tell me she's a lot more than that. Hopefully I can get her alone at some point and ask her about her past, how she kept up in a world dominated by men.

It's been a long day of seeing sights—the London Eye. Piccadilly Circus, and Trafalgar Square—and the sky is a haze of lavender and orange.

We're approaching Audley Square when Royal stops walking and turns to us. "I think I'll say goodnight. It's been a long day."

"You don't want to see the KGB lamppost?" I ask, incredulous.

"I've seen it before," he says wearily.

"Your loss," I say.

Royal reaches out and ruffles my hair.

I swat him away before smoothing it down with both hands.

"Night, Dad," Clarity says, moving toward him for a short hug. They break apart and Royal smiles down at her, chucking her chin.

"Good night," the boys chime in.

Royal gives them a wave before turning to Julep. "You'll keep them out of trouble?"

Julep winks. "I'll do my best."

"I'll take it," he says, signaling for a cab.

Julep leads us across the street to a tall, black lamppost.

I circumvent it, eyeing its metal trunk, looking. "Awesome," I say when I find what I'm looking for. "Guys, come look at this."

My teammates crowd around as I point at the small box on the back of the lamppost.

"What are we looking at?" Vale asks.

"Is this it?" Clarity runs her finger over the painted metal.

"Yep," Julep chimes in, peering over my shoulder. "The KGB lamppost."

"KGB lamppost?" Lotus asks. "Huh?"

"During the Cold War, Soviet operatives working here in London used this lamppost to pass messages back and forth. They'd make a mark with chalk to let each other know there was a message waiting. Pretty cool, huh?" I turn to my teammates, grinning, arms crossed.

"Definitely," Vale says, looking into my eyes. "We need a secret lamppost back home."

I'm about to speak, but Lotus beats me to it. "That would be awesome. We should definitely find a drop spot somewhere in the hotel, outside the Tower."

"Tower?" Julep asks, confused.

"That's what we call our home base," I say, filling her in. "The Ivory Tower. It's from an 80s movie that Clarity and I were obsessed with as kids."

"*You* were obsessed," Clarity chimes in, ruffling my hair.

"Okay, I was obsessed," I concede.

Lotus cuffs my arm. "I always wondered why we called it

that, since it's actually a basement."

I shrug. "Nostalgia." The truth is, we lived in a quaint, three-story brownstone until just after I turned twelve. Royal decided that if his girls were going to follow him into the espionage business, we'd better have a more private living space. That's when he moved us into the Ivory Tower. Sometimes I still miss the window seat we had in our old house. I spent so much time there reading when I was little, and one of the only photos I have left of Mom is of her, curled up in that window seat, face buried in a book.

Vale breaks into my thoughts. "I know you've been wanting to try cockles, so let's go find some."

I look up into his eyes, nodding slowly. "Okay."

His brow furrows slightly. He must see the sadness in my eyes, but he doesn't say anything else. Instead, he turns to the rest of the group. "Who else wants some cockles?"

"No, thank you," Julep says, pointing over her shoulder. "I think I'll head back. You all stay out of trouble, okay?"

Clarity smiles. "Promise."

Julep eyes the boys. "What about you two?"

"Actually, I'm pretty stuffed," Lotus says, patting his stomach. "I'll walk you back."

"Thanks," Julep says. "Night everyone."

They retreat down the sidewalk away from us, walking several feet apart. I might be imagining it, but I think I see Lotus drifting toward Julep as they disappear around the corner.

I turn to Clarity. "You in?" I ask.

"Definitely," she says, and heads off down the street in search of the tiny clams.

When she isn't looking, Vale takes my hand, putting pressure on my palm for just a second.

I look up at him and smile, wishing I could kiss him right now. But it'll have to wait. I shoot off down the street after Clarity, calling over my shoulder. "Come on."

Vale whoops and trots after us.

It's really, really late when Clarity and I unlock our hotel room door and stumble inside in the darkness.

"They're going to have to roll me onto the plane," I say, holding my stomach.

Clarity looks me up and down. "Pretty much."

We collapse onto her bed and burst into laughter. Today was amazing, and tomorrow we're going to Sicily. Clarity hasn't said anything, but I can tell she's bursting at the seams. She can't stop smiling, and her body is ripe with energy. Plus, she unpacked and repacked her wigs three times earlier, which tells me one thing: she's definitely ecstatic about this trip.

I'm going to do her one better. I'm going to scour that island, and if Clarity has any biological family left, I'm going to find them.

Chapter 15

"Be cautious. Keep a low profile." They were the last words Royal said to me before Clarity and I boarded the plane to Palermo, and as I step off the bus into the market, I know that will be a problem. Locals float by in their light, breezy clothing, and tourists tramp over the pavement in loud colored prints and woven, wide-brimmed hats and visors.

I'm definitely overdressed in my black on black. I need to remedy that, blend in to the surroundings. The last thing we need is undue attention.

I turn back to look at Clarity, whose statuesque form hasn't moved from the foot of the bus stairs. She is completely still but for her eyes, which rove over the street market in front of us. Relaxing her shoulders, my sister meets my gaze. Her long, graceful fingers reach out and take my hand. "I'm home," she whispers. With her free hand, she removes the brassy blonde wig from her head and stuffs it into her cross body bag. I've never seen her treat a wig so carelessly before, but I understand why she is doing it. Clarity has longed to return to Sicily for as long as I can remember. Even when Royal brought her to D.C. at eighteen months old, the first words she said in English were, "Go home." I didn't understand then how important it was to have roots in a place, to have somewhere that one felt completely at peace and relaxed, where one could let down their guard without worrying about reprisals. But here—the streets of Palermo—is home for Clarity. Or at least it was when she was a little girl.

The narrow, stone-paved streets are lined with stalls, and vendors walk about offering samples of their mouthwatering eats. The air is filled with the warm, savory scents of street food wafting from carts that dot the marketplace, and the light sweetness of fresh fruits and vegetables. To my left there is a pile of red, orange, and yellow bell peppers gleaming in the sunlight. On the other side, octopuses are arranged in an eight-pointed star shape, their tentacles turned upward to the sky. Clarity relaxes into fluid motion, her movements smoothing out as we walk through the market, her eyes taking in all of the different delicious foods on offer. We stop at one stall to breathe in the tantalizing smell of deep-fried rice balls, and the street vendor grins. "Your first time here?"

Clarity simply stares at him so I nod. "Yeah, we're thrilled to be here." The Texas accent I'm affecting for the duration of our visit to Palermo sounds awkward and cheesy to my ears, but I go with it.

The vendor snatches up two small rice balls, folds them in a napkin, and hands them to us.

"Thank you." I unwrap the treats and offer them to Clarity, who takes one gingerly and begins to nibble on it. Her eyes widen and she pops the remaining half into her mouth.

"This is delicious," she says, beaming at the street vendor. Her accent is better than mine. She's always had an ear for them. After Vale joined our team, Clarity unwittingly picked up his Alabaman accent and couldn't shake it for several days.

"Grazie," the local man says, smiling from ear to ear.

I fish my wallet out from under my shirt, where it's suspended by a cord around my neck. and fumble for some paper money. I can't remember the last time I've used it, but the street vendor holds up a hand. "No need." He holds up his cell phone, which has a mini facial scanner attached over the camera.

"We'll take six."

He holds the device a few inches away from my face, so I hold still until the phone beeps twice.

He returns the phone to wherever it was stashed under his cart and wraps six more rice balls up for us.

"Grazie," Clarity says, still smiling.

The vendor points at her. "Very good."

We munch on our snack as we weave in and out of the stalls, marveling at all of the products available. We are about to sample some street pizza when I notice a kid about 12 lurking between the stalls, and follow his gaze. He's watching a middle-aged couple as they walk through the market pointing and laughing enthusiastically as little things here and there that catch their fancy. They're probably about 60 years old, and obviously tourists. The man is wearing a bright green Hawaiian shirt and khaki shorts. His balding head shines in the sun. The woman's thin, dyed blonde hair is curled over her visor and her purse dangles over one shoulder. It wouldn't be hard for the kid to snatch it, especially if he's got a leather strap cutter stashed somewhere on his person.

Clarity puts a hand on my upper arm and gives a slight shake of her head. "Remember what Dad said."

I bite my lip, still watching.

The boy sneaks up behind the couple and deftly lowers his hand into her purse. He flicks it out again in less than a second, gripping her wallet in his hand. As he's pivoting away from his victim, that's when he spots me. Our eyes lock and he freezes in the middle of the marketplace. His eyes widen in surprise at being caught red-handed. There's no hesitation before the boy bolts off in the other direction. I send a stern look at Clarity. It's not in me to let something like this slide.

Clarity gestures with one hand. "Go. I'll cut him off."

I sprint off after the boy, pumping my arms and legs to reach top speed. My trenchcoat billows out behind me like a superhero's cape. So much for not drawing attention to ourselves.

The boy has an advantage on Loveday: familiarity with the marketplace. He zigs and zags between stalls, dodging shoppers and vendors alike, his sandaled feet slapping the pavement, the wallet still clutched in his hand. But even so, I am gaining on him. Someone yells in Italian as I pass, but I don't understand it. Vale's the linguist, not me.

The boy rounds a cart piled high with onions, knocking them over as he passes. I leap over them to keep from stumbling, and run after him, my trench coat whipping at the backs of my legs.

He glances back at me with large eyes. He mutters something in Italian and puts on a burst of speed.

I can't let him get away.

My eyes rove over the market as I run through it. Everyone is staring at us. This isn't exactly what Royal had in mind. I consider stopping, but it's too late. Tons of eyes are on me. I might as well finish what I started.

The boy rounds a corner and runs smack into Clarity. He falls backward and hits the pavement, dropping the wallet.

I scoop it up and stow it safely with mine under my shirt. Then I bend down and help the boy up, keeping a vise grip on his arm. I can't wipe the smug look off my face. I feel a little like a superhero. "Let's find the local authorities, shall we?" I smirk down at the boy, whose shoulders slump in defeat.

Clarity simply nods and falls into step with me as I turn back toward the marketplace.

The boy halts in his steps, his feet so heavy they could be growing roots down into the pavement. He bites his lip, then looks up at me. "Do you know who my grandfather is?" His voice barely reaches my ears, and his fingers reach up to tug at a lock of his curly, ebony hair.

"Does it matter?" I stare at him, and he shifts his weight from one foot to the other. He crooks a finger, beckoning me to lean down. I don't have far to go. My 5'2" is only a couple inches more than he's got on him.

"My grandfather runs this place."

"What is he, the President?" I chuckle as I straighten up.

"He's in la nostra società."

My entire body tenses. Without standing up straight, I scan the marketplace. A local man skirts around us, averting his eyes. In fact, everyone is conspicuously avoiding looking at the boy, Clarity, and me.

I drop my hand, freeing the kid's arm.

Without a word, he takes off running down the narrow street, passing vendors without noticing, his body light like a leaf caught up in an unruly breeze. But right now I'm thinking Clarity and I are the ones who should be running.

Chapter 16

"What was that about?" Clarity turns from watching the boy's retreating back, eyeing me curiously.

"Not here," I say in a low voice. "Let's return the wallet and get off the street." Getting out of the open may not do much good. I don't know what that boy's grandfather will do if he finds out about our chance meeting, but I doubt he'll have much trouble finding us.

It takes us only a minute to locate the hysterical owner of the Coach wallet I have tucked into my jacket. As I withdraw it and deliver it to the blonde woman, who now has mascara smudges under her eyes, I'm even more aware of how out of place I look in my head-to-toe black and gray coat. Clarity looks much more the part in her ivory blouse, olive green slacks, and leather sandals. And wearing her hair loose was a good choice. She fits right in here.

"Thank you so much," the woman blubbers at me as she presses some money into my palm.

"You're welcome." I turn and walk away across the market, my movements purposefully smooth and inconspicuous. "Why don't we go back to that clothing shop we saw near the bus station?"

Clarity grins. I'm not much of a shopper, since I can order pretty much whatever I want online, but my sister loves shopping in person. She thrills at digging through clothing racks looking for just the right item. She slings her arm through mine and pretty much drags me back up the street toward the boutique. "This is going to be fun," she purrs.

It doesn't take us long to find something much more suited to our time in Palermo. I step down onto the cobblestone street having traded my usual uniform for a white button-up blouse and long khaki shorts. With a relaxed breath, I consult my watch. "Let's find our apartment."

Clarity follows me as I march off down the street. Her eyes rove back and forth, taking in as much as possible in the short time it takes us to find the address. We walk under a huge stone arch held aloft by white stone pillars and into the building's courtyard. Tile stairs arch up toward the second floor on our right. I crane my neck to look at the ceiling, which is an intricately detailed painting of the sea. Seagulls fly overhead, and the water is dotted with small fishing boats.

"It's beautiful," Clarity breathes.

"Hello," comes a voice from an older woman who is walking down the stairs. Her dark hair is streaked with gray and pulled back into a low ponytail. Her white linen frock floats around her as she comes toward us. "Are you the young ladies arriving today?" she asks in lightly accented English.

"Yes." I give her our names, and she leads us to a small office, where she consults a tablet. After verifying our identities, she gives us a room key. "You've got the best room, on the top floor."

Clarity grins at her. "Thank you!"

We head toward the stairs. I climb quickly, focused on finding our destination.

Clarity follows behind, running her fingers along the rough, stone wall.

The staircase has tan walls and cerulean blue tiled steps in a mosaic pattern. It's charming.

Once we reach the landing, I look around. There's only one door, so it must lead to our apartment. The key slides easily into the lock and the door knob turns.

Clarity gasps when we step inside.

The apartment is a studio with a queen-size bed on one side and a couch on the other. A two-person dining table sits near a window overlooking the ocean. The kitchen consists of a two-burner stove, a toaster oven, and a coffee maker. It will do while we are here. I have plenty of money for food. But what causes Clarity to clap her hands in delight is the balcony. French doors open out onto a terrace that looks as if it's suspended out over the ocean. The water is cerulean blue as far as I can see, and the sun sparkles off its ripples like twinkling stars.

Clarity slips across the room and sinks into one of the bright orange folding chairs on the balcony, her eyes fixed on the water. A deep sigh eases out of her.

"I'll be right back."

She nods as I leave the apartment and head back to the bus station for our bags. I'll need to borrow one of her wigs for the rest of our trip.

"I'm back," I say as I enter the apartment, careful to lock the door behind me. I drop the handle on Clarity's suitcase and it falls over. "What have you got in this thing?" I call to her.

She turns, smiling sheepishly.

"Books," we both say together.

I stow our suitcases against the wall, and, after making sure our weapons cases are still locked up tight, I slide both of them under the bed.

"Come sit." Clarity gestures to the orange chair beside hers.

I step into the fresh air and lean out over the balcony to scan the floors below us. Most of the windows are open wide to receive the cool breeze off the water.

"Keep your voice down," I whisper once I'm seated. "We need to talk about the boy."

Clarity looks at me, a quizzical expression on her face. "Why did you let him go?"

I pause, looking out over the water, before looking back at her. "Did you know there's still an active mafia here in Sicily?"

Clarity's face clouds. She shakes her head.

"They manipulate local businesses into paying fees for their protection, control government officials with bribes, that sort of thing. The boy said his grandfather was one of them."

Clarity lowers her eyes to her hands, which are folded in her lap. "So you let him go."

I nod. "Royal said to keep a low profile, and I'm pretty sure that includes, 'Don't piss off the mafia.'"

"Why didn't he just tell us that?" Clarity folds her feet under her and tucks her chin into her hand. Her wavy brunette hair falls forward over her cheeks.

"I don't know, but I'm pretty sure he didn't think we'd start off our trip by catching a mob-connected pickpocket. We'll have to be more careful."

Clarity gives me a small smile. "Surely the boy's grandfather won't waste time on us."

"I hope not." I sit back in my chair and breathe in the humid, salty air.

Later, once I have changed into different attire—a tiered, white linen dress that floats around my shins and a straight, strawberry-blonde wig that reaches my shoulders—Clarity and I once again step out into the street. We walk for a few blocks through the city toward the civic buildings. From the research I've done, it appears that they still keep their birth records in paper files. The city's government building looms up ahead of us, large arches of white stone leading within.

We step inside the building and are greeted by a woman sitting at a low desk.

"Good afternoon," the woman smiles at us. Her accent is pronounced, but pleasing to hear.

"Well hello," I croon in my Texas accent. "My friend was born here seventeen years ago, and we are wondering if we can get ahold of her birth certificate? She lost it in a move."

"Of course," the woman nods, turning to Clarity. "Give me your official identification and I will go look for it."

Clarity fishes her passport out of the pouch around her neck and hands it to the clerk.

I'm confused, though I remain silent. Why would Clarity give the woman her fake passport? It won't help find her real birth certificate.

The woman's eyes widen, but she says nothing. Instead, she reads over the passport several more times. After a moment, she looks up at Clarity. "Arnoni?"

It makes sense now. My sister brought her real passport, along with the fake one Royal assigned to her. Antonia Arnoni is my sister's real name. Of our team, Clarity's real name is the only one I actually know, other than Royal's. A tingle goes down my spine at how little I know about the people to whom I entrust my life on a daily basis. What if one of them turned out to be disloyal? The thought burrows down inside me, though my face remains blank.

"Yes," Clarity nods.

"I'll get this for you right away." The clerk scurries through a wooden door to the back of the building, glancing over her shoulder at us several times as she goes.

Clarity leans toward me."Did you get the sense she's afraid of us?"

It's not a gut feeling, it's the honest truth. She's terrified of us, but I don't know why. Surely she hasn't heard about our run-in with the mafia already. I'm sure news travels fast here in Palermo, but not that fast. It has something to do with Clarity's real name. I turn to my sister. "Something about your name spooked her."

We wait in silence for the woman to return with Clarity's birth certificate. I watch people out the window, some hurrying past, others meandering through the street. It's both a peaceful exercise in observation, and a way to keep alert. The last thing we need is some of the boy's family coming for a visit unannounced.

Clarity sits in a lone wooden chair in the corner and picks up an Italian magazine to flip through it, lingering on some pages more than others.

The door to the back creaks open and the woman hurries toward us, but her hands are empty. "I'm sorry, I wasn't able to find it. Please don't be mad."

"Mad?" Clarity stands and approaches her. "Why would I be mad?" Her face scrunches up.

The woman frowns. "I will keep looking for it and will let you know as soon as I find it. Where can I reach you?"

I pick up a pen and paper off the counter and write down the number of the burner phone I brought with me. "Call us anytime." I hand her the paper and give her an easy smile. "See ya later."

Clarity and I return to the street.

I press my back against the building and scan the marketplace, but see nothing that catches my attention. "Let's go back to the apartment. We need to do a little digging."

Clarity nods and follows me through the street, focusing on the path ahead.

I, on the other hand, can't help but watch over my shoulder.

Chapter 17

"Apparently the Arnoni family is the largest family in the mafia here in Palermo," I say as I look up from Clarity's tablet and meet her eyes. Her face is pale and her mouth forms a small O of surprise.

"I can't believe Dad didn't tell us." She slumps in her chair.

"Maybe he didn't know."

The eyebrow raise I get in response is enough to stop me from continuing along that vein. "I can understand why he would want to keep something like that from you." I reach out and pat her knee. The gesture feels awkward somehow, like the truth about Clarity's origins has built an invisible wall between us. "Don't let this ruin you. You are not them."

"Thanks." She squeezes my hand, but her face is drawn. She stands, smoothing out the wrinkles in her slacks. "I think I'll take a nap." She curls up in the center of the bed and pulls the woven, multicolored blanket up to her shoulders.

My eyes flit to the ocean waves, and are transfixed by their soothing, repetitive creeping toward the sand, followed by a hasty retreat. I'm still for a few minutes until the quiet in the apartment alerts me that Clarity is asleep. Then I stand and cross to my duffel bag, pulling a cell phone out of an inner pocket. I return to the orange folding chair on the balcony and ease myself into it. At the touch of the screen, the phone glows. I send a text to Vale, who is the only person who knows I brought a burner phone to Palermo.

Me

Just found out that Clarity's parents were probably in the Sicilian mafia.

Vale

Are you serious? Are they dangerous?

Me

Look up la nostra società. I'll wait.

My phone is still for several minutes before vibrating again.

Vale
They sound scary. Please be careful.

Me
We will.
But I'm surprised Royal didn't warn us.

Vale
Me too. How is Clarity taking it?

Me
She was pretty shocked. She's napping right now.

Vale
No surprise there. Ha.

Me
Right?!

Vale
What are you up to?

Me
Enjoying the quiet since Lotus isn't here making
noise.

Vale
Ha.

Me
You?

Vale
Julep talked the kitchen staff at the hotel into letting
me observe them. It's awesome.
You should see how fast
they work.

Me
That sounds right up your alley.

Vale
You're up my alley.
That sounds dirtier than I meant it to be.

Me

Lol.

Vale
Have to go. Miss you.

Me
Miss you too.

After my conversation with Vale, I open a document on Clarity's tablet and write out a list of recommendations about how Darnay can improve the security around his valet service at his hotels. For a former spy, his anti-theft protocols are pretty lax. I send it off to Royal, then sit, staring out at the ocean, keeping an eye on the street below. Now that I know about Clarity's birth family, I'm basically on guard duty.

In the morning, Clarity and I find a cute little café right down the street from our apartment. Red planter boxes filled with bursts of colorful flora line the large, clear windows. A hand-painted, wooden sign over the door reads La Panetteria. My stomach lets out a growl as we walk up the cobblestone street toward the open doorway. I've been awake for a while now, waiting for Clarity to get ready, and I'm starving.

We step inside and are greeted by the smell of freshly baked bread and pastries. A young woman, not a lot older than us, gives a welcoming smile from behind the counter. "Good morning."

"Morning!" Clarity says in response, pressing close to the glass case to take in all of the baked goodies.

I decide what I want and ask Clarity to order for us, once she's chosen an item or two. Then I turn to watch out the windows. The streets are fairly busy even at this early hour, with shop owners and vendors straightening their places of business. Commuters march past the bakery toward work, while others stroll through the streets, coffee in hand, enjoying the quiet of early morning. I try to stifle a yawn, but can't. Truth be told, I would have preferred to sleep in but Clarity woke me up at the butt crack of dawn so she'd have someone to talk to while she put her makeup on.

I'm biting into my first powdered-sugar-coated pastry, called a "virgin's nipple," and trying not to snicker, when a large man in a bright white button-up and gray tweed shorts walks into the shop, followed by two other equally bulky, scary looking men. A quick glance over their persons reveals that the first man is unarmed, but the other two each have a shoulder holster hidden under their roomy, linen button-up shirts.

I reach down toward my waist with one hand, my fingers inching toward the handgun I've got concealed under my shirt, not taking my eyes off the three men as they stroll toward the counter and order their breakfast.

The only other patron of the café, a man that I take to be a fisherman from his clothing and distinct scent, casts a worried glance at us before standing and exiting the shop, clutching his coffee cup in his hand.

The young woman behind the counter pales. She works at a fast pace, her movements jittery as she serves them. Once they have their food and drinks in hand, the three men turn toward us.

I'm praying they'll walk right past us, but of course that's not what happens.

Clarity glances up from her pastry and locks eyes with the first man, her body tensing.

He smiles somberly at us before sitting in the one free chair at our small, round table. After taking a sip of his steaming hot coffee, the man speaks. "Welcome to Palermo. I'm Beppe Arnoni."

The name confirms it; this guy is in the mob.

I remain still. Maybe, if I don't make any sudden movements, he'll realize we aren't his prey.

Arnoni seems unphased by my silence, and takes another unconcerned sip of his drink. "I heard you had a run-in with my grandson yesterday." He sets the still-steaming cup down on the table and folds his hands in his lap, waiting for a response.

Clarity looks at me, her eyes full of worry.

My arm is draped casually in my lap, but my fingers are inches from my gun holster. I'm confident that if I need to, I can draw before these three goons can reach for their weapons.

"It was simply a misunderstanding." I meet the man's eyes, my face blank. I hope he buys my Texas accent. Even if he doesn't, it's too late to drop it now.

"A misunderstanding, eh? I was told you planned to take him to the police."

I keep my body relaxed, casual, like Royal trained me to do. "He stole a woman's wallet." It sounds as if it's no big thing, like a comment about the weather.

The man levels a steely gaze at me, and lifts one hand to rub his temple. "Don't trouble the police with small matters such as this. We will take care of it."

I nod. "I understand." I understand by his tone that he means, 'Keep your mouth shut, or we will take care of you.'

"You visited our local government building yesterday. I trust you found the information you needed." He studies me, his focused brown eyes not blinking.

Clarity slings one arm behind her back to where she keeps her handgun at the small of her waist.

I put a hand on her shoulder and squeeze. "We did. Thank you."

The man gives a stiff smile and stands. "Maybe we will meet again." In other words, 'We'll be watching.' My eyes are trained on Arnoni and his two companions as they leave the shop, but they don't spare us another look.

Clarity leans toward me and puts one hand on my forearm as it rests on the table. "Was that who I think it was?"

I glance over toward the service counter, but the young woman who greeted us is nowhere to be seen. "The mafia, you mean?" I say in a low voice. "Is Lotus a Cubs fan?"

She breathes out, nodding.

I lean toward her, catching her eyes. "Look, I know we just got here, but I don't think we should stick around."

She deflates, slumping over the wrought iron table and nibbling at her pastry before responding. "Can we at least go to the hall of records again? If she still hasn't found my birth certificate, then we can go."

"My thoughts exactly." I don't know what will happen if our new gentleman acquaintance finds out that Clarity is a legacy mafia member, and I'm not waiting around to find out.

Chapter 18

But when we reach the government building, they aren't open yet.

Clarity groans as she turns to me. "They don't open for another hour." She looks out over the water. "Want to take a walk down the beach?"

I follow her gaze, watching a few fishing boats bob up and down on the rippling waves. "Okay." We take off our shoes and walk down the sand at the water's edge. The clear, cool liquid ripples around our toes, beckoning.

"I wish we had time to swim," Clarity says, her lips turning down in a pout.

"I'm sorry." It's way too cold to swim this early in the morning, and by the time it warms up this afternoon, we'll be gone.

The records office still isn't open when Clarity and I again walk up the steps to its front door, so we head back to our apartment.

I give them a call as soon as we get inside, and after a couple tries, the woman we spoke to yesterday answers. She still hasn't found Clarity's birth certificate. It's not anywhere in their records. The office worker is still apologizing as I hang up. "They don't have it."

"That's odd," Clarity says from the floor, where she's scrubbing off the remains of bright blue nail polish from her toes. "Do we have time to go swimming before we go?"

I shake my head. "I think we should leave. Now."

She continues rubbing a blue-stained cotton ball over her toenails, not looking up at me. "I know, but we just got here. This is my first time in sixteen years."

I crouch down beside her, watching her long fingers as she works. "We can't wait around for la nostra società to visit the records office and figure out who you are. I don't know what they'll do when they find out."

Clarity sighs. "You're right. I'll get my things."

It doesn't take me long to gather my stuff, so while my sister packs, I send Royal a message.

> **Me**
> **We're heading your way.**

> **Royal**
> **Did you find Clarity's family?**

> **Me**
> **Yes and no. Will explain when we get there.**

> **Royal**
> **Travel safely.**

> **Me**
> **Will do.**

We're on a plane in less than three hours, but this time we're crammed into coach, and not even sitting together. We took the last available seats on the plane. Clarity's up front, and I'm near the middle. I lift myself off the seat so I can see her. She's slouching down in her seat, so I just catch a glimpse of the top of her head, her brassy blonde wig back in place.

I settle down in my seat, put in my earbuds, and turn on the television that's inset into the back of the seat in front of me. I might as well continue my Marvel movie binge.

Chapter 19

The lights are just beginning to twinkle when our plane touches down in Kuala Lumpur. The wide patches of lush green grow darker, impenetrable. A thrill runs through me. It's really happening. I'm being paid to fly to Malaysia to do a job. For a client. As a spy. I can't keep the smile from rising to my lips. Up until now, I've only worked for clients around the U.S., mostly corporate types. But on this trip alone I've visited two countries already, and the third is right outside our airplane door. This is when the real adventure starts.

I catch up to Clarity as she walks down the ramp away from the plane, and give her an exuberant tap with my elbow. "Hey."

She gazes down at me, a sad smile on her face.

My body sags at the pensive look in her eyes. "I'm sorry we had to leave so fast. It sucks."

Her lips flatten. "I understand it, but it doesn't make it easier." She drapes an arm over my shoulders and leads me through the airport. I slide my hands into the pockets of my coat so they don't constantly bump against Clarity's side, my bags slung over my other shoulder. We weave through the crowds, past the baggage claim area and toward a set of large glass doors. Just beyond the doors, there are cars, buses, trucks, and limousines inching past.

"You looked up a schematic of the airport?"

She's smiling now. "Yes." We sit on a bench outside and wait. Clarity pulls out her tablet and studies satellite maps of Kuala Lumpur and Port Klang.

I consider taking my copy of *The Enchanted Castle* out of my bag, but a car pulls up just as I'm reaching for it.

It's Lotus driving a black sedan. He waves at us with one hand, an easy smile on his face.

Julep is sitting in the passenger seat, and rolls down the window. "Do you need any help loading your bags?"

I look down at our bags, my duffle bag and weapons, and Clarity's large rolling suitcase, then back at Julep. "Nope. Thanks." Honestly, it's a shock to me that they let Clarity carry on her suitcase, but she can be pretty charming when she wants to be. By the time she finished talking to the ticket agent and wafted away toward security, he was starry eyed.

We load our bags in the trunk of the sedan before sliding into the back seat, me behind Lotus and Clarity behind Julep, since it'll afford her more leg room. Lotus is only 5'10", but he sits so far back in the seat when he drives he's practically laying down.

Julep grins as she twists in her seat to greet us. "You have no idea how glad I am that you two are here."

"What, you're tired of being the only girl in a sausage fest?" I laugh.

Clarity lets out a low, short laugh, her eyes scanning everything outside her window.

"You could say that," Julep says.

"Hey, hey," Lotus says, feigning indignation. He smooths one hand over his short, curly hair and pulls out into traffic.

I watch him as he drives confidently through the darkened streets of Kuala Lumpur, the city lights illuminating our faces in oranges, reds, and blues. He falls into driving in different places so easily. It's part of why Royal recruited him. I'm a pretty capable driver, but I wouldn't be able to pick up and go as easily as Lotus does.

My eyes turn to the back of Julep's head. I tap her shoulder. "Can I ask you a question?"

She turns to smile at me. "Ask away."

"Why Julep? You got a thing for bourbon?"

Julep's laugh is loud and brassy. "Tell me, what do you think of when you hear names like Cookie and Barbie?"

"Bimbo trophy wife?"

She shoots a look at me. "Pretty harsh."

I slide down in my seat a bit. "Sorry."

She wags a finger. "No, that's exactly what I'm getting at. People underestimate women with frou-frou names like that. When men hear my name, they don't expect me to kick them in the balls and confiscate their weapons in 1.2 seconds. But that's exactly what happens."

"Nice," I say, pumping my fist.

"It's a problem, people being judged by their names, and I take advantage of it. In this game, you take every advantage you're given. Understand?"

"Hell yeah."

Despite my training, my mouth gapes open when I catch sight of our room. The bed is on the only solid wall. The other three walls are glass, and the lights of the city stretch out below us. The streets are awash with red and white lights as cars buzz through the city center.

"Your dad said you wouldn't mind sharing again," Julep

says at our backs.

"This is amazing." Clarity sighs, giving Julep a big hug.

"I'm right next door if you need me," Julep says, and sees herself out.

Clarity flops down on the bed and spreads her arms and legs wide. "So, where are you going to sleep?" She grins.

"Gee, I don't know," I trail off, dropping my duffle bag and bending to set my hardshell briefcase on the ground. "Right here!" I run and leap, landing on top of her, tickling her sides until she can't breathe through her laughter.

"What's going on in there?" Vale's voice floats through the door.

Lotus chuckles. "It sounds like someone is dying."

It's true. Clarity is fairly squawking with laughter.

We sit up, faces red. "Go ahead," she says, nodding toward the door. "Let them in."

As soon as the door is open, Lotus and Vale whoosh into the room.

"Welcome back," Vale says, giving me a casual side hug before plopping down in one of the two cream-colored, roll arm chairs in the corner.

"Thanks!" Clarity says, brightly. She spreads out on her side on the bed, propping her head on her hand.

"Isn't this fantastic?" Lotus says, gesturing to the view outside our window. "It's going to be hard going back to living underground."

"You're not wrong," I respond, my eyes gazing out at the city.

"You should have seen Sicily," Clarity sighs. "It was beautiful. I only wish we could have stayed longer."

"About that," Royal says from the doorway. "Loveday, can you step outside with me for a minute?" His sandy brown hair

131

is getting long, the ends creeping down over his ears. "Clarity," I say over my shoulder. "Come with us. Bring your clippers." I meet Royal at the door and turn, waiting for my sister.

"Will do." She digs around in her oversized suitcase and comes up with a small, black zippered case. "Anyone else need a trim?"

Lotus's hand flies up to his short afro. "No, I'm good." Clarity cuts all of our hair, except his. Lotus insists on going to a barber. It makes sense, though. Clarity has pretty much no experience with natural black hair.

"Hurry back," Vale says, still lounging in the chair, a smile playing on his lips. "We want to show you Alor Street."

"Yes!" Lotus licks his lips. "I'm starving."

My stomach rumbles as Clarity and I follow Royal down the hall to his hotel room. We haven't eaten since breakfast, and all they gave us on the plane was a small bag of chips.

Clarity sets up a folding chair on the mottled travertine floor in the spacious bathroom. "Ready?" she chirps, clippers poised in her hand.

Royal pulls off his black button up and sits in the chair in a white tank. "Ready." He twists in his chair to look at her. "Actually, just take a little off the sides, okay? I kind of like the top a bit longer." He turns forward again, his hands resting on his knees, his back straight as a board.

Clarity's eyes flit to me. "Trim it all," I mouth to her. The clipper buzzes to life and she works her way around Royal's head, from left to right, starting around his ear.

"So, how was Sicily?" he says over the low buzz. His cool blue eyes meet mine.

"It was… surprising," I say, standing in front of Royal with my hands in my pockets. "They couldn't find Clarity's birth certificate."

Royal crosses his left leg over his right, his foot balanced over his knee. "Really? That's odd."

"Uncross your legs, Dad," Clarity says without looking up.

"Sorry," he says, straightening out.

Clarity's trimming the hairs on Royal's neck now, her eyes focused, slender hands steady.

I shift on my feet. "I thought so," I say. "And it gets more interesting. Clarity's birth name is Antonia Arnoni, right?"

Royal nods. "And you know not to share that with anyone." It's not a question.

A ripple runs through me. This is starting to feel more like an interrogation than a debrief.

"Of course." I pause, studying my dad's face. It's curiously void of emotion. An idea hits me, but it's absurd. It couldn't be. I ask anyway. "Did you know that the Arnonis are a part of the mafia there in Sicily?"

"I did."

"So, you were just hoping we wouldn't find out? Is there more you haven't told us?"

Royal's face remains blank. There are no traces of emotion, and no attempt to defend his chosen course of action. And that's when I know: there's more that he's hiding.

Chapter 20

I'm still working to slow my racing heart as Clarity and I meet the boys at the elevator. Vale pushes the button and we climb inside. I soak in their excited energy, letting it overtake my cynicism about Royal. I can revisit that later. Right now I want to enjoy some time with my teammates.

"You're going to love this," Vale says. "There are so many types of street food it's unbelievable."

"I hope you're hungry," Lotus says, patting his stomach.

"I could eat," I say, my eyes flitting to Clarity.

She's standing facing the glass wall of the elevator, her back to us, her eyes taking in the lush greenery and neon lights on the street below.

"You have to try the chicken satay. I know we've had it at restaurants back home, but it's not even close to the same thing." Vale rubs his hands together like a little kid in a toy store. "It's amazing."

Once we hit the street, Vale leads us up the sidewalk. We turn a corner and there it is. The street is lined with brightly lit booths, each displaying large photos of delectable-looking food dishes. Red lanterns are strung all along the street, creating a twinkling canopy over the entire area. Low concrete pillars block off the road so cars can't drive down it. Instead, the space is littered with red and white plastic tables and chairs, packed together to accommodate the most people.

My eyes go wide. "Wow."

"You're not kidding," Lotus says. He grabs Clarity's elbow. "Come on. You've got to try the stuffed pancakes, and the flatbread, and the meat kabobs." He pulls her up the street, weaving through clusters of people.

"Meet back here," I call after them, but I'm pretty sure they didn't hear me.

Vale steps up beside me, and I'm keenly aware that we're alone. His fingers weave through mine. A warm tingle runs along my arm and I smile up at him. He gives my hand a light tug. "Come on."

But my feet are like lead. "Wait."

Vale turns back to me, his eyes questioning.

"Come here," I say, beckoning for him to bend down.

He does, a sly smile forming on his mouth. One hand snakes around my back as Vale moves in to kiss me, but I put up a hand to stop him. "Not that." My heart beats a fast rhythm in my chest. "Can you do something for me?" I whisper in his year.

Vale's green eyes catch mine. "Anything," he whispers back.

I take a deep breath, squeezing his hand. "I need you to hack into Royal's laptop. There's something I need to find."

Vale's eyes go wide, and he doesn't say anything for a minute. He simply stands there, looking down at me, his face inches from mine.

I don't break away. "Can you do that?"

Then, he gives a slight nod of his head. "Yes."

Our bodies still, the weight of what I've just asked him

heavy between us.

"Thank you," I say, pulling him down for a light kiss. My stomach growls. "Let's get some of that delicious food you've been raving about."

The sun is just peeking over the horizon, its first rays cutting through the morning haze. Lotus, Clarity, Vale, and I are on our stomachs on top of the container terminal near the largest shipyard at Port Klang, an hour and a half outside Kuala Lumpur. Each of us has a pair of binoculars up to our eyes, studying the dock that runs along the water's edge. There are huge blue cranes all along the dock, and stacks and stacks of shipping containers span the length of the coast.

"There are plenty of places to hide," I say, lowering my binoculars.

Vale does the same, and our eyes meet.

"What did Royal say when he brought you guys out here?" I ask.

The corners of Vale's mouth turn up. "That it'll probably be easiest to nab the thumb drive once the shipping container is unloaded, before the crew moves the cars to whatever chop shop they're taking them to. He'd rather we didn't tangle with the locals."

I scan the shipyard. "That shouldn't be a problem. I can get in and out of that car in a few seconds since there's already a hole in the moon roof. Once it gets closer to the ship's expected arrival date, we'll start monitoring the satellite feed around the clock until the ship arrives. That way we won't miss it."

Clarity nods in agreement.

I pull up to a crouch. "Everyone ready to go?"

Beside me, Vale uses his binoculars to scan the coastline.

"Anyone up for a trip to see some mangroves?"

"Me," Clarity says. "I bet they're beautiful in person."

"I'm down," Lotus says, standing.

"Sounds great," I say as I stretch my arms over my head to relieve the ache in my muscles. "Make sure you don't leave anything."

While my teammates are scouring the rooftop, I walk over to the maintenance door and peer down the stairs. "It looks clear," I say, glancing over my shoulder toward my teammates. "Let's move."

I tap on my watch to send Royal a message.

Me
We're leaving the park now. Want us to pick up breakfast?

I smirk as I type. If anyone ever got ahold of my watch, they'd think I'm a typical teenage girl who spends her time shopping, sightseeing, and eating. That's the idea, anyway. They might think I'm addicted to take out, which is kind of true, at least when I'm away from the Tower. No matter where I am, I like to sample the local flavor instead of the food at whatever hotel Royal has us booked into. It's much more interesting that way, even around the U.S., where most of our work has been up to now.

My hand hovers over my belt as we make our way down the stairs, my fingers ready to unholster my tranquilizer gun at the first sign of movement. It's after 07:00, but the sun is just now rising, so although the port is buzzing with activity, there isn't a lot going on inside the maintenance stairwell. We get outside to where we parked our motorcycles without incident. Lotus and Vale mount their respective bikes. Clarity slides onto the back of mine, and we head back toward Kuala Lumpur.

The freighter isn't scheduled to make port for another week, and we have a lot to do in the meantime.

My skin feels sticky from the humidity as we park our motorcycles outside the hotel and waltz into the adjacent restaurant. Royal and Julep are sitting in a corner booth, facing the door. I'm not surprised. Royal never sits with his back to a room. He says it's a security risk. I would say that he's slightly paranoid, but some of the veiled references he's made to his spying days make it more than plausible that there might be someone out there with a grudge against him. Royal smiles as he catches my eye.

Julep grins and waves us over.

I lead the team to meet them, stepping aside to allow Clarity to sit next to Royal before I slide into the booth. Across from me, Lotus is sitting suspiciously far away from Julep, leaving Vale perched on the edge of the bench seat. Lotus adjusts, elbowing Vale in the ribs.

"Ouch," Vale says, frowning. "I think I'll get a chair." He does so, which leaves him sitting with his back directly to the main part of the restaurant. Unlike Royal, Vale is at ease this way since he doesn't have years of espionage work, and possibly even enemies, at his back. Of course, if anything does happen, there are five sets of eyes keeping watch.

I look at Royal, who is alert, watchful. I relax and look down at the breakfast menu.

I'm digging into my buttered toast with jam, soft-boiled eggs, and creamy hot cocoa when Julep speaks up. "What do y'all have planned for today?"

Royal glances at her before returning his attention to his oatmeal. It's piled high with butter, brown sugar, and banana slices. "I've secured an empty lot for some training exercises.

138

You're welcome to come, if you wish."

Julep smiles widely. "That sounds great. I'd love to see everyone in action."

Lotus ducks his head and bites into his cold cereal, but he's blushing. Crap, I think he's got the hots for Julep. That's going to be super complicated, and he should know better. But then guilt rises up in me and I give myself a mental shake. Double standard much? I shove down any irritation and focus on my breakfast.

We eat in companionable silence for a few minutes, while everyone is focused on their breakfast.

After a while, Vale takes a long swig of water, then speaks. "Will I be using your laptop to run the comms for the training?" he asks Royal. His eyes shift to me and back. His ears are tinged pink. Hold it together, Vale. If he can get ahold of Royal's laptop for even a few minutes, he'll have a chance to scope out whatever firewall Royal has installed that partitions the software we use for comms from the rest of his apps and files. This could be our in, a way to dig into the information he has on my sister.

Royal chews his food for a moment, thinking. "No, there's no need for that today. I want you in the field for this." He gives Vale a closed-lipped smile to avoid showing a mouthful of see-food.

"Nice, man!" Lotus offers his fist, and Vale responds halfheartedly, his eyes cutting toward me.

I smile. "That's great," but my delivery is flat.

Beside me, Clarity takes a sip of her frothy tea. "Welcome to field-work," she says after swallowing. Her eyes are alight.

Vale shifts in his chair, trying to suppress a grin. He goes still when our eyes meet.

Royal catches the exchange and leans forward to make eye

contact with me past Clarity. "Is that all right with you? I know we didn't discuss it."

I wipe my mouth with my napkin before responding. "It's fine. Vale will be a real asset in the field."

"It's settled then," Royal says. The table goes quiet as we finish breakfast.

My mind is churning. My instincts fight my brain. I know that Vale will, after more training, be a great field agent, but then he won't be safe. It'll be a mental effort to avoid worrying about him when we're all in the field, which is why I'm positive Royal would frown on any and all romances between members of our team. I bite down on my toast, savoring the crunch as it hits my tongue. He might be right.

On the other hand, having Vale in the field will increase the amount of protection Lotus, Clarity, and I have when we're working. We'll be able to split into neat teams of two. But it'll prevent Vale from hacking into Royal's laptop, maybe indefinitely. I go back and forth between scenarios, unable to nail down exactly how I'm feeling about Vale joining us in the field. Normally making decisions is easy, cut and dry, but not this time. Royal may think this discussion is settled, but in my mind it most definitely is not.

Chapter 21

"We'll meet you four at that address in an hour," Royal says, gesturing to our watches, which all chime at the same time. I glance down at the address he's sent us.

"No problem. We'll round up our gear."

Julep gives me a toothy smile. "I'm really looking forward to this. I've been curious about you guys ever since Mr. Darnay mentioned you months ago."

I didn't know that Mr. Darnay had been talking about us to Julep, but I don't tell her that. Instead, I give a polite nod, then turn toward the bank of elevators. Clarity skips ahead of me, pushing the button to summon one.

Behind me, Vale and Lotus are chatting about what paintball guns they're bringing for training today.

The elevator doors slide open and I freeze, listening. Two women are arguing in the hallway, the tension between them cutting through the air. My hand goes to my side, where my tranquilizer gun is tucked into a holster inside my belt, under my loose black tee. I glance at my teammates, signaling them to fall in behind me. I peek out of the elevator and scan the hallway. The yelling is in Japanese, and it's coming from the direction of our rooms. Silently, I step out of the elevator, keeping my back to the wall. I advance toward the raised voices, poised to act.

Clarity follows me, Vale her, and Lotus brings up the rear. Clarity and Lotus both hold a hand over their holsters. Vale, who doesn't typically carry a weapon, has his phone out, his fingers racing over the touch screen.

It's obvious to me as we approach that the yelling is coming from the boys' room, based on the housekeeping cart that's sitting in the hall outside their door. I turn to Lotus and mouth, "Your room." He nods in return and slinks forward to stand beside me, his dominant hand still at the ready should he need to draw his gun.

"Wait," he breathes, putting a hand on my shoulder. I halt a few feet from his hotel room, not taking my eyes off the passage ahead.

"I think that's Haru and her mom," he whispers. "Let me check." Just as he steps forward, a lithe girl, her straight, brunette hair up in a tight ponytail, bursts from the room, a glare on her face. The neat hairstyle, tan dress, and bright white sneakers she's wearing signify the fact that she's on the housekeeping staff here at the hotel. She shoots a look behind her before she sees us. Her eyes go wide, but her surprise at seeing us melts when she sees Lotus. "Lotus, sorry," she says in accented English.

"Don't worry about it," Lotus says as he steps toward her. His face hovers a few inches above hers. "You all right?"

She nods. "My mom." She gestures toward the room, where a vacuum can be heard coming to life. "I have to go." She takes hold of the housekeeping cart and moves off down the hall, entering the next room with her key card.

The vacuum shuts off, and a short Japanese woman marches out of the room, her finger raised. She stops when she sees us, her face austere. "Almost done," she says, before sweeping past us and into the next room.

This time I can hear two voices murmuring in Japanese. They're clearly arguing while trying to remain quiet so we can't hear them.

I turn to Lotus. "Who is that?" I lean forward to peek into his room. The vacuum is standing in the middle of the carpet, but everything else is sparkling clean. I raise my eyebrows as I turn back to him. "You know her how?"

"We caught her arguing with her mom up here the first day we arrived."

"They're fighting about Haru's schooling," Vale interjects, his face turning pink as he speaks. "She wants to study computer technology, but her mom wants her to study business and get into the hotel trade here in the city."

"She told you all of this?" Clarity asks, peering past him down the hall.

Vale's face is bright red now, and he fidgets with his hands, clasping them and dropping them again.

I smirk. "No, she didn't." He was eavesdropping, in Japanese. Maybe he'll make a good field agent yet.

When we pull up to the lot on our motorcycles, I can see why Royal chose it. The entire lot is overgrown with banana plants, elephant ear plants, various types of palm trees, and shrubs with bright yellow, orange, and red flowers. There's a wide dirt road that cuts into the foliage at the edge of the lot.

"Wowza," Lotus says, dismounting from his bike. Turning to me, he grins, pulling at his black athletic shorts. "Glad I wore black instead of my usual red."

I chuckle. "Glad I wore boots instead of my signature sneakers." I look down at the black combat boots. They're much more suited to the humid, overgrown environment that surrounds us.

Clarity slides off the back of my motorcycle, pulling her skinny black jeggings, which rode up her thighs during our drive, back down to her ankles. She adjusts her black tank before standing up and gazing over the plot.

Vale sidles up beside me, catching my eye. "Is this outfit okay for this?"

I look down at his charcoal tee, black knit pants, and boots. "Like I said before we left the hotel, as long as you wear dark colors and avoid fabrics that make noise, you're going to be fine."

Clarity reaches up and slings an arm over Vale's shoulder. A slow smile rises on her lips. "This is going to be fun."

A small hatchback approaches, slowing as it comes even with us. Royal pulls the car into the dirt at the side of the road and gets out. Julep slides out of the passenger seat and comes around the car to lean against its hood. I don't know how she's going to play paintball with us in a cream blouse, pencil skirt, and heels, but I don't question it. From what I've seen so far, she can handle herself.

"Let's find a better place to park our bikes," I say, meeting Royal's eyes. "Maybe over here." I stride over to the dirt path and peer down it. There's a clearing up ahead. "Let's move our stuff up there."

Royal nods and gets back into his car, steering it expertly up the path. Lotus, Vale, and I follow on our bikes. Clarity and Julep trail behind, chatting.

Royal pops the hatchback open and motions toward the interior of the car. "Put everything you won't need in here. I don't want anything valuable left on those bikes."

"Yes, sir," I say, retrieving a small weapons case from the

storage compartment on the back of the motorcycle. Removing my handgun from its holster at my waist, I tuck it safely inside, along with my folding tactical knife and my karambits. My hand hovers over them for a second before I snap the case shut and lock it. I stow it in the back of Royal's car, beside Lotus and Clarity's cases. Vale's case is smaller, as the only thing in it is a Smith and Wesson 640 series revolver and some ammunition. He's going to have to put a lot more time in at the shooting range before he does any serious fieldwork.

Julep retrieves a case out of the passenger seat and flips it open in the trunk of the car. With deft, practiced movements, she starts pulling weapons and clips out from various parts of her person. She slides a Glock 17 and two extra clips out of a corset under her blouse. A Smith and Wesson MP and extra clip come out of a holster strapped to her inner thigh, along with a nasty-looking folding knife. Lastly, she unbuttons her cream blouse and drapes it over the locked case, revealing the black camisole she was wearing underneath. She turns and catches me grinning at her.

"Wow," I say, raising my hand for a high five.

She smirks. "Always have to be prepared." She disappears behind the car and returns in a moment, having exchanged her knee-length pencil skirt for black yoga pants and her stilettos for black sneakers.

"Gear up," Royal says, and we prep our various paintball weapons, ammo, and goggles.

Clarity pulls two black knit caps out of the storage bag on the back of our bike and hands me one. She pulls it down over her wavy brunette hair, the ends sticking out in all directions under the cap. I pull mine on over my bleached blond faux hawk and grin at her. Once my paintball rifle is loaded, I speak. "Ready?"

She nods, clutching her paintball pistol to her chest. "Definitely." Royal stopped insisting Clarity use a paintball rifle years ago, because she easily bested us all when she used one. Now, with the pistol, Clarity shoots rarely, and never misses. This, combined with her ability to move without making any sound, makes her a daunting opponent.

Vale hesitates when Royal takes his paintball rifle and instead offers him a paintball pistol. "Um, you want me to use this?" he asks, his voice higher, glancing from the gun to Royal and back.

Royal taps his chest with the pistol. "It'll make you more careful about when you shoot, and force you to be more accurate, since you're starting at a disadvantage."

Vale takes it in one hand, a look of frustration on his face. "Yes, sir."

Royal gives him a pat on the shoulder. "Listen. Focus. You'll be fine." Then he turns to the rest of us. "Here are the teams: Loveday, Lotus, and myself versus Julep, Vale, and Clarity." He motions to the dirt beneath our feet. "This path runs all the way around this lot, and that's the boundary line. If you are hit, sit down where you are and wait for the exercise to end. Last team to have a man standing picks where we eat dinner tonight." He grins. "And I'm in the mood for curry." He cocks his rifle. "Form up. You have two minutes to strategize. Use them wisely."

We separate into our respective teams, huddling up. "Curry sounds delish," Lotus says. "What's the game plan?"

I look past him to the playing field. It's totally flat, and there's a grouping of tall, overgrown trees near the middle of the lot that will provide excellent cover. None of the trees are good for climbing, though. "I vote we make for the trees and stand facing outward. The foliage in the area should provide plenty of cover, and that way we can see them coming from any direction."

Lotus and Royal nod. "Agreed. Let's go."

Clarity's team is walking up the road, presumably looking for the opposite boundary line. I keep one eye on them as Royal, Lotus, and myself melt into the foliage, making our way toward the cluster of trees. My steps are measured, slow. I'm doing my best to avoid making noise, but no matter how deliberate my movements, I can't seem to maneuver without brushing against the twigs and leaves of the plants around me. I pause to listen for the approach of the other team, but hear nothing.

We reach the trees, and Lotus and Royal position themselves facing outward on either side of a large ironwood. Their eyes scan the playing field. Giant elephant ear leaves provide a screen they can hide behind.

I scan the undergrowth and spot a huge elephant ear plant on the other side of the tree. It's perfect. I crouch and crawl past Lotus, pushing under the huge leaves toward the center of the plant. The ground is damp, but there's room for me beneath the plant's wide foliage. I adjust my beanie to make sure my hair is covered, then wriggle onto my stomach on the soft, moist ground. I rub some of the mud on my cheeks so that my pale skin doesn't stand out, and wait.

A paintball rifle is fired somewhere to my left, toward Royal. He crouches, half hidden behind a couple of young tree ferns, and fires back.

It's silent.

I take several deep breaths to keep my heart rate down. It's just a training exercise, and I use the opportunity to practice remaining calm under stress.

To my right, a paintball pistol fires.

Lotus swears loudly as he ducks down. The paintball hits the tree trunk just over his shoulder with a splat. "That was a close one," he whispers.

"Pay attention," Royal warns.

I say nothing. If it's Clarity who took that shot, she's close by, and I don't want to give away my position.

A cluster of paintballs comes screeching toward Royal, and he ducks further down, shooting in response.

Again, silence reigns. We haven't hit any of them, and they're getting awfully close to eliminating Royal and Lotus.

I don't dare move as a shower of paintballs paints a swath of neon blue across Lotus's chest. "Oh man!" He throws his arms up. "I'm out," he says, sitting down with his back to the tree, his rifle across his lap.

There's a brush of movement through the foliage at my left, past Royal. He takes aim and fires without hesitation.

A groan reaches my ears. "You got me," Julep says, her voice echoing through the trees.

One down.

I scan the undergrowth around the trees, but I don't see Clarity creeping up on Royal until it's too late.

"Royal. Your nine!" I yell, but Clarity nails his left shoulder.

He grins at her. "That was magnificent," he says at the same time that I fire my rifle.

Paint splatters across Clarity's butt as she attempts to melt back into the foliage. She spins around in surprise, but I don't think she can see me through the huge leaves of the elephant ear plant I'm lying under.

A breeze plays at the back of my neck. It's a relief from the hot humidity of the earth beneath me, but I'm surprised it's able to get through the thick, rubbery leaves surrounding me.

Wait.

The sound of a paintball pistol being cocked hits my ears and I twist around.

Vale is holding the leaves above me aside with one hand, his pistol aimed right at me.

My eyes widen as he fires, and neon blue paint hits my chest. "Ow," I groan. "That's going to leave a mark." I wipe at it with one hand.

"I got you," Vale says with a surprised look on his face. "Are you okay?" he says, quieter.

I push off the ground and stand, dusting the dirt off my clothes. "I'm fine. Nice job."

"So that's where you were hiding," Julep says as she pushes a branch aside and walks toward us. "We spotted Royal and Lotus but couldn't find you. That is, until you shot Clarity."

I tilt my head, shrugging. "I had to take the risk."

"Luckily, I was right behind you and didn't know it," Vale says. He reaches toward my face with one hand, brushing at the dirt smudges on my cheeks. "Camouflage?" he asks, voice low.

I stiffen at his touch. Everyone is watching. "You know it."

Clarity's voice snaps us out of it. "We win," she cheers gleefully from her spot a few feet away. She grins, moving toward us. "Vale, that was amazing."

"Thanks," he says, giving her a high five.

"Yeah, lucky," Lotus says, giving him a fist bump.

We huddle up and Royal gives us a few tips and things to watch out for the next round. "Okay, new teams. Let's do girls versus boys this time."

"Excellent," I say, giving Clarity a shoulder bump.

She turns to Lotus and Vale with a sardonic grin. "You

ready for this?"

By the time we've played a few more rounds, we're all covered in splotches of brightly-colored paint. From the soreness in my skin, I know I'm going to have several really attractive welts tomorrow.

"This was fun!" Julep says as we make our way back to where we parked our vehicles. "We'll have to do it again sometime." She loosens her hair and pulls the box braids forward over her shoulder so she can inspect them for paintball residue. Finding none, she flips them back into place with one hand.

Royal leads us back to the clearing where our vehicles are parked. "Nice job today, everyone. We'll meet in the hotel lobby for dinner at 7, and we'll go from there. Girls, think about where you want to eat."

"Oh, we will," I say, lifting my watch to my face. "Now, where's the priciest restaurant in the city?"

"Within reason," Royal says.

"Fine," I say in mock disappointment.

Clarity threads her arm through mine. "Up for a swim?"

I nod in the affirmative. "Sounds amazing." We turn in our paintball gear and hop on my motorcycle, heading back to the hotel with Lotus, Vale, Royal, and Julep trailing behind us.

On our drive back, I replay the training exercise in my mind. Vale snuck up on me. It's true that he didn't know where I was, so hitting me was part luck, but it's also true that I didn't hear him coming. So either I wasn't alert enough, or Vale is sneakier than I thought he could be. And I don't know which one is worse.

Chapter 22

"Hey!" Lotus calls from the hallway.

Clarity pulls the straps of her white bathing suit over her shoulders and makes for the door.

I scramble to get my bikini top in place before it swings open.

"Did she leave you extra pillow mints too?" Lotus bounds into the room wearing offensively bright neon blue swim trunks, a towel slung over his shoulder. He holds out his hand, palm up, to show us a fistful of dessert mints. He strides over to the king-size bed Clarity and I share and peers at our pillows. "Ha! She left me more than you." He points at me and heads for the door. "Pool, ten minutes?"

"We'll be there."

Lotus nods and makes off down the hall.

I turn to Clarity. "It looks like someone has an admirer."

A sly smile plays on my sister's lips. "I'm sure he's enjoying the attention. Under all that bluster and bravado, he's still human."

It catches me off guard, the idea that Lotus needs confidence boosts like the rest of us. He's always seemed so self-assured to me. But as the idea settles I know Clarity is right.

I turn away from her, holding up my SPF 50 sunblock. "Can you do my back?"

The four of us meet at the pool, jumping in to see who can make the biggest splash. Lotus wins, of course.

After a game of water volleyball, Lotus claims a floating raft and falls asleep on it.

Clarity pulls herself out of the pool and stretches out on a lounge chair for a nap.

Vale moves through the water toward me, keeping low. He puts a hand on my waist under the water. "Hey," he whispers.

"Hey," I whisper back, glancing over to make sure Lotus and Clarity aren't watching us.

"Do you think you can sneak past Clarity tonight? Meet me in my room?"

I smile, the idea warming me through. "Definitely."

And you know what? I pull it off. Once she's asleep, I ease out into the hall and down to Vale's room.

He smiles when he opens his door, his hair ruffled.

"Were you asleep?" I ask. "I can go back…"

"No way." He pulls me into his room and closes the door.

I move through the darkness to the window to peer down at the cars zooming down the streets below, their headlights are flashes of white on the pavement. No matter how many times I see this view, it never gets old.

Vale takes my hand. "Come on," he says, pulling me toward his bed.

He climbs onto the big bed and stretches out over the comforter.

I creep across the carpet after him, crawl onto the bed, and curl up on my side facing him. "You were amazing today," I whisper.

A grin spreads over his face. "Thanks. It felt good." He turns to look at me. "I'm ready to be out in the field with you guys. I want to be there, in case…"

I reach out and rest my hand on his chest. "Nothing's ever going to happen. We're highly trained, and most of our missions aren't that dangerous anyway."

"You call sneaking onto a cruise ship to nab one of the performers right off the deck a cake walk?"

I wag my finger at him. "It *was* pretty fun." But the guy didn't pose a threat. He was just someone who'd stolen the wrong person's identity, and we'd been hired to bring him back so he could be charged.

"Technically, I think kidnapping someone from a cruise ship makes you a pirate."

"I'm a regular Mary Read."

Vale turns to face me and slings his arm over my side, his forehead furrowed. "Didn't she die in prison?"

"Well, yeah, but that won't happen to me. We don't break the rules; we only bend them, and only with permission from the CIA." I reach up and run my fingers through his hair. "You have to promise me that you'll be careful once Royal puts you in the field. I can't be worried about you when we're on a mission. I can't have my focus divided."

He breathes out, closing his eyes at my touch. He reaches up, catching my hand. "I will be. You won't have to worry about me, at least not any more than you do Lotus or Clarity."

"Have you seen Clarity? She could sneak up on someone who was staring right at her." We both laugh, but it's definitely true.

"She's so quiet. How does she *do* that?"

"I don't know. I can't do it, no matter how much I will myself to be silent."

Vale scoots closer, his breath warm on my skin. "Have you thought any more about, you know, telling your dad about us?"

I look away, toward the clock on the nightstand behind him. I know what Royal would say: he would require us to break up, and he'd make sure we didn't spend any alone time together. And he'd never let Vale in the field. His warnings about controlling my emotions on the job rumble through my brain. *"Emotions are messy. You have to be detached, logical. If you're not, you'll make mistakes. And then someone will get hurt."*

"Loveday?" Vale's voice is a whisper on my face as he leans forward to kiss me.

I duck and his mouth lands on my ear.

"Sorry," he says with a chuckle, repositioning for another attempt.

I shake my head. I can't stay. Maybe Royal is right; dating someone on my team is a mistake. "I have to go." Before Vale can get a word in, I'm out the door.

Chapter 23

Guilt coils in my stomach, making it impossible to sleep. I open my eyes and lift my wrist in front of my face and tap the screen. A low glow illuminates the screen. It's on night mode, which is supposed to be easier on the eyes. I debate about what to say to Vale, but decide the direct approach is best. Well, mostly direct.

Me
I'm sorry.
I shouldn't have left like that
This mission has me wound up tight.

Vale
:(
I wish you'd talk to me instead of shutting me out.

Me
Sorry, again.

Vale
It's okay.
Once we complete this mission, we can tell everyone, and you'll feel much better.

Me

> **You sure about that?**
> **Sneaking around is kind of fun.**
> **Plus it's good practice.**

Vale
Ha.

Vale sends me a couple Captain America memes, and I have to smother my mouth with my hand to suppress the giggles that bubble up inside me. I manage not to wake Clarity, but I can't stop smiling as I fall asleep.

Lotus dragged Vale along on his search for a shot glass to add to his collection, so it's pretty quiet in Royal's hotel suite.

Clarity and I are sitting at opposite ends of the couch, reading. I'm working my way through an Ultrawoman graphic novel and my sister is reading a Malaysian fashion magazine she picked up at a kiosk on the street. Occasionally she tears out a page or two which are destined to be hung up outside our dorm room back in the Ivory Tower.

In one of the roll-arm chairs facing the couch, Julep sits, legs crossed, knitting a pair of socks with soft, crimson yarn. She says it's her favorite thing to knit because her feet freeze during London winters.

Across the room, Royal is sitting at the narrow walnut desk, working on his laptop when his phone rings. With a quick glance at us, he bustles out of the room, away from our eager ears. He's probably talking to Darnay again. That man is sure antsy to get that thumb drive back. Royal's evasiveness about the phone calls has me at high alert. Something is going on.

Royal's evasiveness about his conversations with his friend has me wary, but I trust him. He's always been honest with Clarity and me, as honest as he can be given the restrictions the government puts on his past life. It's partly why we call our home the Ivory Tower—it's our escape from the disheartening reality that people are often disappointing. Of course, we didn't realize that when we started calling it that at twelve, but as my sister and I have gotten older and observed more of the dark corners of the world, the name has become more fitting.

I turn to meet Julep's eyes. "What's that about?"

She watches Royal leave the room before meeting my gaze. "I don't know." Her lips purse together. "When I've spoken to Mr. Darnay, he's made it obvious that he would rather be here with us than taking a tour of his hotels, but he's been planning this trip for months and didn't want to renege on his commitments."

"Right," I say, nodding.

"And, I think he's going to stop in to see his son as well," Julep adds casually.

Clarity must pick up on it as well, because she asks, "His son doesn't live with him?"

Julep shakes her head. "He's abroad, at school." She uncrosses her legs and crosses them the other way, then lifts her glass and takes a sip of iced tea. She's finished talking about Darnay's personal life.

I take her cue and change the subject. "How did you get into intelligence?" I ask, propping my elbows on my knees and leaning forward onto my hands.

Julep smiles widely.

"I went into the police academy at eighteen," Julep says, licking her lips. "I had always wanted to be a cop, to improve the system from the inside."

Clarity cocks her head. "And?"

"I was really good at undercover work." She lets out a short laugh. "I ran into a CIA operative while I was on the job.

Sean. He liked the way I thought, so he put in a good word for me. I joined six months later, and was with them for a year, until Sean was killed." Her countenance changes; it's heavier somehow. "Then I wanted out."

I frown, my lips pursed. "Sorry."

Clarity puts a hand on Julep's shoulder. "That must have been awful."

Julep gives us both a small smile. "It was." She smooths her violet linen skirt. "How did you girls get involved in spy work?"

Clarity and I look at each other, grinning. "Shall I?" My sister asks.

"Definitely."

"We overheard Dad planning a simple bump and grab, and we beat him to it."

"She bumped, I grabbed." I can't help but laugh at the memory: Clarity wearing her first wig, a shoulder-length, russet red number with curled ends, and oversized sunglasses. Her gangly limbs and big eyes made her look like a stylish insect. And I came behind in my muted colors, my naturally brown hair down and brushing my shoulders. I hadn't yet discovered my love for platinum blond spikes. "Tell her the best part."

"What's the best part?" Julep leans in, curious.

"We were eleven. And the wallet we stole? It belonged to a traitorous secret service agent. Royal found the number of a Russian agent inside."

"Wait, are you guys talking about that agent..." she trails off, searching for the name. "Cobb? It happened what, six years ago?"

Clarity and I both nod. "Yep," I say.

"Smooth," Julep says, eyeing us both. "So that makes you what? Eighteen?"

"Almost." I push my hair off my forehead. "My birthday is in a couple months. Clarity's is three months after that."

"Hmm. When you two turn twenty-one, I owe you a drink."

"Way to go." Royal's voice floats over the waist-high partition that separates my shooting gallery from Vale's. He claps Vale on the back before unclipping the paper target and taking a good look at it. "You've improved a lot in the last several months." Vale smiles. He's doing a marvelous job of pretending he's not frustrated with me for leaving him last night, but I can see it in the line of his shoulders and the way he's avoided looking at me all morning. I'm surprised Royal isn't picking up on the tension. Or if he is, he's keeping any comments to himself.

"Loveday, are you finished?" Royal's question jolts me to attention. He's watching me.

"Almost," I say, facing forward again. I lift my gun, holding it securely in both hands, and empty the clip into the black and white cardboard cutout of a man standing thirty yards away. The shots echo in my ears, even through my protective earmuffs.

Royal's phone goes off, for the third time since we arrived at the shooting range, and he hurries down the hall away from the shooting gallery. He takes a quick glance back at us before moving around the corner to answer the still-ringing phone.

My eyes narrow. Either it's almost killing Darnay not to be here, or there's more to the story than we've been told. I make sure my gun is unloaded before setting it down and creeping down the hall toward him.

"Something's up," Clarity says over my shoulder.

I jump at her voice. "Geez, Sis."

She smiles sheepishly. "Sorry."

I motion in the direction Royal went, and Clarity nods in understanding. Together, we edge down the hall. As soon as his voice is discernible, I stop, pressing my back to the wall.

Clarity bends down to tighten the laces on her sneakers, strands from her silvery-gray wig falling in her face.

Royal's voice floats toward us, tight and clipped. "Charles, we're ready to get the drive back as soon as the ship docks... No. We already decided an oversea mission isn't feasible. Remember?" His voice trails off as he listens to Darnay. "Don't worry; they won't ever know it was misplaced. I promise."

I turn to Clarity, eyes wide. Darnay sounds pretty desperate to get that thumb drive back. The information on it must be more important than Julep has said. Either that, or she doesn't have any idea what's on it either and was just repeating what Darnay told her about its contents. "Let's move," I mouth to Clarity. Royal can't catch us eavesdropping on him. I'd like to think he'd be proud of how good we've gotten at gathering information without being detected, but I'm not about to field test my theory.

We move back up the hall toward the shooting gallery. Vale and Lotus are huddled together in Vale's lane. Lotus is monitoring Vale as he reloads his gun. "Nailed it," Lotus says with a smile, thumping Vale on the back. His eyes lift to catch mine, and he raises his eyebrows. I wink in response.

I slide in beside him, and Clarity hovers beside Vale. "Darnay isn't telling us the whole story," I say, before leaning back to catch a glimpse of Royal coming toward us, still on the phone. "There's sensitive information on that thumb drive, and Darnay will be in hot water if whoever gave it to him finds out it's missing."

"What do you think it is?" Vale asks. It's the first thing

he's said to me today, but he still doesn't quite meet my eyes.

"I don't know, but we have to find out."

"What's the plan?" Clarity asks, arms crossed lightly over her chest.

Standing there, with all three of them looking down at me, it strikes me how short I am. Like, really short. It's not something I think about often. I shake off the thought. I need to focus. "I'm tempted to come right out and ask Royal. As far as I know, he's never lied to us before."

"True," Lotus says. "He's always been straight with me."

Clarity and Vale bob their heads in agreement.

I take one more peek down the hall. "Okay, I'll ask him. If he won't tell me, we get more creative."

I pull Vale aside as we're preparing to leave the shooting range. Lotus and Clarity are down the hall packing up their gear, and Royal is in the front office talking to the man behind the counter. "Hey." My fingers barely fit in my jean pockets, but I keep them there anyway. Stupid tiny pockets. I look up into Vale's face. "Are we okay?"

He clenches his jaw for a moment before meeting my gaze. "Yeah, we're okay." My stomach flips at the way he's looking at me.

"I'm sorry. Maybe after we're done with this mission we can tell him. I just…" I trail off, hoping Vale will finish the thought. He doesn't, so I continue. "I just know that if Royal finds out about us, he'll insist we break up. He may even boot you from our team, and I don't want that." I take his hand, rubbing my thumb over his fingers.

"Me either," Vale says. He leans down and gives me a gentle kiss.

I inhale deeply. "Your shooting was awesome today, so

precise."

He smiles. "Thanks." His body stills, and he speaks quieter. "About that other thing. I haven't had any luck getting through the partition on Royal's laptop." He glances down the hall to make sure Lotus and Clarity aren't in sight. "I set up an app that will break through and send me a notification when it's done. I can have it send you one too. That way we'll know when we're through and I won't have to keep coming up with reasons to use the laptop."

"Please do." As I'm speaking, the hairs on the back of my neck prickle, and I swivel around to make sure we aren't being spied on. I don't see Lotus or Clarity anywhere. Still, I don't want to stand here any longer. "Let's go; Royal's probably waiting for us." We carry our weapons cases out to the main office, where Royal is almost done settling up with the proprietor.

"Meet me outside," he says over his shoulder. "I'll be right there."

Vale holds the door open for me, and I step out into the humidity. But I freeze when I see who's waiting for us in the parking lot.

Clarity and Lotus are already there, and I have no idea when they passed us in the hall. Or how much they may have heard.

The van beeps, signaling that it's been unlocked, and Royal brushes past me. "Let's go."

I stiffen. Does he know about Vale and me too? I curse myself. I've gotten careless, sloppy. I glance up at Vale, whose face is pale. He gulps.

We slide into the van in silence.

Clarity and Lotus are in the back, Lotus playing a game on his phone. Clarity's nose is already deep in a book—*The Color*

Purple by Alice Walker. Without looking up, she reaches forward and taps my shoulder.

I turn, and she holds out a tiny slip of paper. I breathe it open in the hopes that Royal won't hear the paper crackling from the front seat. Still, it creaks. Clarity's written on it in her neat, scripted hand.

We need to talk. Tonight.

My eyes scan the words quickly, and I fold up the paper.

"What is that?" Royal asks from the driver's seat, not looking back.

"Gum," Clarity and I say together. I cast around for somewhere to discard the paper, but the interior of the van is an exercise in spartan design. Knowing my pockets are too small to hold pretty much anything, I shove the paper into my mouth and chomp it to bits.

"Want a piece?" Clarity adds, snark in her voice.

"No thank you," Royal says. He meets my eyes through the rear view mirror. I make a show of chewing the now disintegrating paper, and Royal's eyes return to the road.

I swallow the wet lump. This is exactly why we don't usually use paper for anything; it's tricky to get rid of. Digital files can be deleted rather than being eaten. I grimace at the gross, chemical taste in my mouth. Now I really do want some gum. I fish a piece out of my utility belt and pop it into my mouth. The strong cinnamon taste is a relief.

Lotus lets out a low chuckle from the back seat.

I look over at Vale out of my peripheral vision.

He's watching me, his hands folded loosely across his knees.

I raise my eyebrows at him and jerk my head toward the window. Catching my meaning, he leans away from me and trains his gaze at the buildings as the van whirs past.

So, tonight is my reckoning.

Chapter 24

Clarity is an ace at pretending nothing is wrong. It's almost as if she were trained to hide her emotions. So when I close the door behind Julep that night, after a tense briefing in which Royal and Julep drilled us on our plan for recovering the thumb drive once the freighter is in port, it's a surprise when Clarity turns on me, her expression hard. "You've been lying to me," she says, stalking across the room and flinging herself down into one of the plush chairs in the corner near the glass wall overlooking the city.

"I'm sorry. I wanted to tell you, but I figured the fewer people who knew, the better. I didn't want to ask you to lie to Dad." My words are whisper thin, transparent. It's true, but the excuse still sounds feeble once it's floating in the air between us.

She shakes her head, crossing her legs, her own voice low. "Knowing you're lying to me is ten times worse than me having to lie to Dad."

I drop my head. "I'm sorry." I shove my hands into my trench coat pockets, relishing the extra room to stretch my fingers.

She levels a withering look at me. "Did you think I didn't

know?"

My mouth drops open. "You knew?"

Clarity's eyebrow rises and she tilts her head to one side, her lips pursed. "Come on, Loveday. We live together, in the same room, in an underground fortress. There's nowhere to hide."

"Does Dad…" I trail off, unable to form the words. If he does know, I'm doomed.

"No, Dad's clueless, but only because until today you've managed to keep your extracurricular activities to the nocturnal hours, and he goes to bed early."

I bring my shoulders down from around my ears. Hearing this from my sister is a huge relief. I let out a loud exhale, but the onslaught isn't over.

Clarity frowns up at me. "You're getting sloppy. We saw you two at the shooting range today. Your emotions are clouding your judgment."

I press my hand over my eyes, frustrated with myself. She's right. I slink across the room toward her and sink into the opposite chair. "I'm so sorry." Even though the arms of our chairs are inches apart, I can feel the void between us, and it'll only grow if I don't do something about it. I reach across and grab her hand. She doesn't pull away, which is a good sign. "What do you want me to do? Break up with him?"

Clarity huffs. "Honestly, I wish you'd never started dating him in the first place, but—"

"It wasn't my plan either."

With a head shake, she continues. "Like I was saying, since it's too late to nip this thing before it gets going, you've got to be more careful. You can't afford to let your emotions continue to affect your decision-making. We all depend on you in the field, and I won't go out there knowing you aren't 100%

focused on what we're doing. Lotus won't either."

I swallow. "He knows too?"

Clarity nods. "He's unsubtly asked me in the past if I thought you and Vale were a thing, but I put him off. I couldn't do that today. He saw you guys, same as me."

I squeeze her hand. "Thanks for keeping it to yourself. You're the best."

"And?" She stares me down, waiting for more.

I sigh. "I'll figure this out. It won't affect my choices in the field, and I won't let anything like this afternoon happen again."

A smile cracks her lips. "Good." She leans forward and gives me a loose hug, but then jerks back. "Why is Vale trying to hack through the partition on Dad's laptop?"

There's no point in holding back now. It's always helped to bounce my thoughts off Clarity, and there's so much I've been keeping from her that I'm aching to tell her. Also, she was right about what she said: lying to her feels much worse than lying to Royal. "Royal knew the Arnonis were mafia before he let us go to Sicily, right?"

"Yes." Clarity's face is tight, pained by this admission.

"There's more."

Her eyes widen.

"I think Royal knew we wouldn't find your birth certificate."

Clarity gasps, her hand flying to her mouth, but she doesn't deny it. Her fixed expression is unnerving.

"Clarity?"

She drags her eyes upward to meet mine. "I called the records office in Sicily again today. They still haven't found it."

I shake my head. "And they never will. I think Royal took it when he adopted you, and destroyed it."

"Why would he do that?"

I cock my head. "Probably so the Arnonis couldn't find you when the mess from the earthquake calmed down."

Clarity's mouth is flat. "Then why would he lie about it?" There's doubt edging her voice, and I know the feeling. We've never had reason to question Royal before. He's been our pillar of virtue, a lone, noble, constant authority figure our entire lives. I lean over the side of my chair and put a hand on her arm.

"That's what I'm trying to find out. I'm betting Royal has a file on each of us in his laptop, and I want to know what's in yours. There's got to be a reason he didn't tell you about your parents, and I want to know what it is."

She wrings her hands. "Me too." A beat passes. "How... how close is Vale to getting in?"

I sigh. "From what Vale has said, Royal's firewall is pretty intense. Vale set up an alert to let us know when the app he installed gets through, but it could take days. Or weeks. And there aren't a ton of reasons for Vale to use the laptop in the first place."

Clarity runs her hand through her hair. "I have to show you something." She leans over the arm of the chair to where her suitcase is propped against it, pulls out her tablet, and opens it. Holding it out to me, she says, "Look in my web browser."

When I open the browser, she's got tens of tabs open, and all of them are articles about the Arnonis. I scan through them, and my heart stops. There's an obituary dated sixteen years ago. Clarity would have been fifteen months old.

Public Funeral Held for Arnoni Family Members Lost in Earthquake

January 14, 2016

Hundreds attended the public funeral today for Carmine (28) and Giada (23) Arnoni. The cathedral in Monreale was packed with people wishing to pay their respects to the family during their time of grieving.

Carmine married Giada in a traditional Catholic service in 2014, when she was just twenty years old. He joined her family's property management business here in Palermo, while she remained at home. They had a baby a year later, in June of 2014, but sadly the baby was lost in the earthquake last month, along with her parents.

Below the headline, there's a color photograph of a young couple in nice clothes, laughing and holding a chubby baby with a head of dark hair. It's Clarity; I'm sure of it. I look up at her to see tears in her eyes.

"My birth parents," she says, her voice trembling.

I wrap an arm around her, gripping the tablet in my other hand. "Are you sure?"

She nods. "The dates line up. I was born in June of 2014. And Dad said my parents died in the earthquake."

I squeeze her to my side. She rests her head against mine, wiping at her wet cheeks. "Wow."

"The only question is, why did they print in the paper that I died, when I didn't?"

I shake my head, my eyes trained on the photograph. "That's not the only question."

I'm stretched out on the bed, reading *The Secret Garden*. Clarity is beside me, curled into a ball, sniffing after having a good cry. Her voice, throaty after her crying jag, creaks in the silence. "Do you ever think about your mom?"

Images flash before my eyes. A car wrapped around a telephone pole, the whole left side of the car crumpled. Blood on a shattered windshield. An empty car seat, the only thing intact in the totaled car. A hysterical baby in her dad's arms. A man's eyes trained on a body draped in a white cloth. My stomach twists. I don't remember the car crash. I was only eighteen months old when it happened, but I've seen the photos. I looked them up on the internet when I was ten, after a fight with Royal about whether or not I should be allowed to train for field-work.

"Your mom would kill me if she knew I let you follow in my footsteps," he had said, frustration edging his usually low, sonorous voice.

"Mom would want me to be able to take care of myself," I'd shot back. I'd stomped into my room and searched her name and the words "car accident." The photos were stark and grisly, but I hadn't been able to look away. They burned into my brain, never to be forgotten. Once you see something, you can't unsee it.

I close my book and look down at Clarity, who's just picked up a book of her own. *The Handmaid's Tale*. "Of course I think about her." Sometimes I can't make it stop. I wonder what it would have been like to hold her hand on my first day of kindergarten, what her laugh sounded like, whether we would have gotten along or fought like crazy. The stories Royal tells about her, when he's in the rare mood to talk about her, aren't enough. They'll never be enough.

Clarity smiles. "You look like her."

The thought warms me. I think so, too, but hearing my sister say so helps a lot. I lean down to press my forehead against hers. "You saved us." It's true. As Royal tells it, he brought Clarity home a mere three months after my mom passed. She became my constant companion, and she gave Royal something else to focus on besides his dead wife and the toddler she'd left behind.

Clarity flushes. "You and Dad saved me right back." She drapes an arm over my middle and squeezes. "I'm so glad I didn't grow up an Arnoni."

"Me too," I whisper.

Chapter 25

Lotus and Vale are in the middle of a good-natured argument when Clarity and I arrive at their breakfast table, which is tucked into the corner of the dining area of the hotel's plush restaurant. I slide in beside Lotus, and Clarity hunkers down next to Vale. I could sit by him myself, since Lotus and Clarity know about us, but I'd rather keep up the pretense.

Lotus takes a bite of a hard-boiled egg, chewing, wagging his hand at Vale. He swallows roughly, and speaks. "Sean Connery is the best James Bond. He defined the role. He was cold, calculating, but hot enough to get the ladies."

Vale rolls his eyes. "He's too smooth. Too perfect. Daniel Craig is so much more believable."

Lotus shakes his head, mouth open. "No. No. Craig is too bumbling, too rough. There's no way he'd make it in the field."

Vale throws his fork down on top of his half-eaten poached eggs and toast. "He's new to it," Vale says. "Casino Royale is about his first mission. He needs time to adjust, get his bearings."

"And he almost dies," Lotus says. "There's no time for mistakes like that in real life."

Vale furrows his eyebrows at Lotus, who reaches for the

plate of fresh fruit in the middle of the table. "Sorry, man, but it's Connery all the way. Has to be."

I look from Lotus to Vale. It's obvious to me by the way Vale is staring at his breakfast that he's arguing about more than James Bond. He's defending himself.

"Loveday will back me up," Lotus says through a mouthful of mango. "Right?"

Clarity's smirking. She knows my favorite Bond, and what will happen if I say his name out loud.

I frown. "I'm not getting into an argument about the best James Bond with you two."

"Come on," Lotus says, bumping his shoulder into mine. "Craig wouldn't last in the field, right? He's too sloppy."

My sister wiggles her eyebrows at me. "Go ahead," she mouths.

I exhale loudly. "He is pretty rough around the edges, yeah. But every agent starts somewhere. Remember your first field mission?"

Lotus scoffs. "That was one time."

I smile at him. "You got yourself locked in the craft closet of a preschool. I had to bust you out."

He grins. "Okay. Okay. You've got a point." He holds out a piece of buttered toast to Vale. "Truce?"

Vale takes the peace offering, but his eyes are sad. "Truce."

I reach for some bacon. "Anyway, you're both wrong about the best James Bond."

Their heads swivel toward me, their mouths open in shock.

I wait a beat to increase the anticipation. "It's Timothy Dalton, all the way."

The table erupts in chaos.

Royal comes into the restaurant and looks around. When his eyes catch on us, he walks over with a smile on his face. "Are you ready for another flying lesson?" He gazes down at Lotus, his blue eyes warm. If I know one thing about Royal, it's that he loves to fly, even with Lotus at the wheel.

"Are you serious? Hell yeah I'm ready." Lotus taps me on the arm, and I slide out of the booth, making way for him to pass. He hops up, grinning. "Let's do this."

Royal nods, turning to me, giving me a meager smile. He looks a little green around the gills. "We'll touch base when we get back."

"Good luck," I call to their retreating backs, before turning to Clarity and Vale. "Think he'll land the plane successfully this time?" I can't help the smirk from rising.

Vale tears his eyes from the door they've just walked through and meets my eyes. "I hope so. He's gotten really good at the simulator." He straightens the hem of his shirt sleeve, drawing my attention to his toned arms. "If he doesn't, I don't see Royal giving him another shot for quite a while."

Clarity whistles, high and clear. "I think you're right."

I hope Lotus sticks the landing this time, for all our sakes.

After breakfast, Clarity excuses herself by saying she wants to visit an orchid greenhouse a few blocks away. She doesn't invite us, which is fine with me. My sister knows me well enough to know that a trip to a greenhouse wouldn't be high on my must-do list. "Don't have too much fun without me," she says over her shoulder, but I catch the sly smile on her face as she looks from me to Vale.

"What was that about?" I ask, eyes narrowed.

"Nothing." The tinge of pink in his cheeks gives him away.

"You're lying to me. Tell me what's going on." Before he can stop me, I've got a hand on his stomach, tickling him mercilessly.

"Stop. Stop," he begs between laughs.

My fingers play his stomach like a piano. "You'll tell me what I want to know?"

Vale nods, unable to talk through his laughter.

"Okay." I pull away from him and take a casual sip of my ice water.

"I asked Clarity if she could think of a way to help you relax a bit, since you're under so much pressure, and she told me about this sweet spa treatment involving cocoa beans. Does that sound like something you'd be interested in?"

My eyebrow arches. "Does it involve a massage?"

"Yes?" His voice rises as he speaks, his hesitance at my response obvious.

"Then yes, I'm interested."

Vale grins now. "Perfect, because your appointment is in…" He consults his watch. "Twenty minutes. Go change into something comfy and get yourself to the hotel spa, missy."

"Missy?"

"It popped into my head, so I went with it. It sounded weird, right?"

I laugh as I lean toward him, pressing my lips to his. "Thank you," I whisper as we part.

"I'll do anything for you," he says. And I'm one hundred percent certain he means it.

My watch vibrates, and I lift my wrist to read the message.

Lotus
I DID IT!

I raise my fist in the air, thrilled for my pseudo brother. It's an effort, because after my morning at the spa I'm feeling so relaxed my body keeps trying to fall asleep.

Vale, Clarity, and I are sprawled out on lounge chairs under a giant umbrella, near the pool behind the hotel.

"That's awesome!" Vale asks. "Pretty soon we'll be able to go on missions without Royal."

Clarity shakes her head, a smirk on her lips. She adjusts her swimsuit. "We'll see."

I, too, have doubts. Just because Lotus has finally learned to fly, and land, a plane doesn't mean Royal will give us permission to go gallivanting around without supervision.

Vale turns his head toward me. "Loveday, do you think he'll let us?"

I raise my eyebrows. The man who until last week always met with our clients alone? "No." At the sight of his crestfallen face, I add, "Not right away, anyway."

This perks him up a little.

I nudge him with my bare foot, and he grins, rolling off his lounge chair and crawling over to me.

He leans down over where I'm lying, face up on my chair, and kisses me lightly, his mouth hovering over mine. "I've been dying to do that in the daylight forever."

"Me too," I breathe. I glance at Clarity, who gives me a small smile before training her eyes on the people walking up the path. She seems uncomfortable with our PDA. Really, I don't blame her. It's weird acting like a couple in front of other people.

Our watches vibrate again.

Lotus
Where you guys at?

Vale sits down with his back against the side of my chair and types a response.

Vale
Swimming pool

I turn onto my stomach and rejoin Clarity in people watching. The pool is dotted with swimmers in various types of bathing suits. Others sit in the lounge chairs lining the water, reading, talking, drinking, or sleeping. It's fascinating, studying how people dress, move, and interact with each other. The little details we catch help round out our fake identities too.

Lotus comes loping across the grass toward us, plopping down on my lounge chair next to me. "We've got a problem," he whispers, holding up his hands over his mouth.

Vale pivots to face us both.

Clarity swings her legs over the side of her chair and scoots it toward mine, enclosing us in a tight space between the chairs.

My watch vibrates again.

Royal
Meeting in ten minutes.

I ignore it, sitting up to give Lotus more room on the lounge chair beside me.

"What kind of problem?"

"Darnay finally told Royal what was on that thumb drive."

I lean sideways toward him. "And he told you?"

"Not exactly." He sends a furtive glance my way.

I snicker. "What is it with this team and eavesdropping?"

Clarity's laughter tinkles. "Occupational hazard."

The look on Lotus's face stops me from joining in. Whatever is on that drive is not funny. "Spill."

"MI6 tasked Darnay with going over the reports for all of the missions during which agents or civilians have died for, like, the past fifty years." His face is ashen.

"And all of that data was on the thumb drive," I supply, my jaw set.

"If anyone else gets ahold of it…" Clarity trails off, her face drawn.

I swallow. It would open up a gargantuan can of worms for intelligence agencies around the world if someone got their hands on those files. First of all, they'd know way more about how the U.S. and the U.K. conduct missions and espionage work than they should. Both agencies would have to restructure their entire protocols for field agents. In addition, if anyone were able to figure out the identities of any of the agents in those files, it would be disastrous. Even if the agents in question are dead, many of them did things in enemy territory that could be prosecuted in a court of law. Heck, I've hijacked a plane and I'm not even an official CIA agent. Agreements of peace between sovereign nations the world over could become tenuous, at best. And the safety of any living agents whose mission logs show up in those files would be compromised. It would be a gigantic mess. "Are their real names in the file?"

"I… I don't know." Lotus shakes his hands out as if trying to rid himself of what he's just told us.

Vale's eyes are on me. "Whoever finds it will have access to mission details, protocols, locations… How hard would it be to figure out the identities of the agents?"

I shake my head. "It would be tricky without agent profiles, but not impossible." I work to control the fury bubbling up in me. Darnay knew vital information and withheld it. What appeared to be a random string of car thefts could have been a play by any number of countries' governments to intercept sensitive data and undermine MI6 and all cooperating agencies, including the CIA and my dad. I wouldn't put it past Russia, China, or even Pakistan. The fact that all of that information is out in the world, up for grabs to the first person who finds it, changes everything. "Let's go." I march across the lawn toward the hotel, my fists clenched. I don't need to look behind me to know my teammates are at my back.

Chapter 26

We only have three minutes before our meeting with Royal, so I should change out of my bikini and into more suitable clothing, but I have to make a stop first. I stalk out of the elevator and down the hall, stopping in front of Julep's door, one hand holding tightly to the towel wrapped around my waist. With my free hand, I knock. Hard.

There's bustling inside, and then the door swings open.

"Did you know about this?" I burst out, pushing past Julep into her hotel room.

Clarity follows on my heels, a mask of calm on her face.

The boys shuffle in behind, looking nervous.

Julep shuts the door behind us and returns to her bed, where her clothing is folded in neat piles beside her suitcase. "Know about what?" She plays with the thin silver band that circles her thumb.

"The contents of the thumb drive."

She picks up one of the stacks of clothes and sets it in her suitcase, pressing it to smooth out the wrinkles. She glances up at me, her eyes worried. "No. Not until a few minutes ago."

I study her. She's not fidgeting, sweating, or averting her eyes. She's either a smooth criminal or telling the truth.

"I believe you," I say, relaxing the tension from my body.

Beside me, Clarity nods. "Me too."

Julep exhales, shooting us a grateful smile. "I never would have tasked you with retrieving the thumb drive if I had known the stakes." Her lips purse.

"Right," Lotus says, crossing his arms.

Julep looks up at him, her expression softening. "I'm sorry, truly, that Mr. Darnay got all of you involved in this." She turns her attention back to her belongings, her body rigid. She's holding it together for our benefit.

"All right then." I spin on my heel and go down the hall to Royal's door. A second after my swift rap on the painted wood, he answers.

The anger simmering under his calm facade is reassuring. He takes one look at the four of us. "You know."

"Yes," Clarity and I say together.

Behind me, Lotus harrumphs.

He steps back and lets us into his room. Clarity settles on the couch and the boys take the plush chairs. The range of emotions coursing through me have me wired, so I don't sit. Instead, I stand with one hand on my cocked hip.

Royal follows us, putting a hand on Lotus's shoulder.

The boy shrinks slightly, unsure of whether he's in trouble or not.

But our normally taciturn leader chuckles. "I'm both proud of your spying skills and angry that you were eavesdropping."

Lotus gives him a timid smile. "Thanks?"

Royal shakes his head, but the anger has drained away from his features. He turns to me. "I've told Charles to send someone else to retrieve the drive. This is too big for you all."

My mind goes back to Julep. The clothing on her bed.

She's packing to leave Kuala Lumpur, and the mission isn't even over.

But it's not in me to walk away and leave something unfinished. Especially this, our first international mission. We've spent weeks, months, and years in training, going on missions all over the United States, and it was all in preparation for this. I stand and take a step toward Royal. "Call him back. Let us finish this. It's what you trained us for."

"We're ready," Clarity adds as she stands up, coming shoulder to shoulder with me. Well, more like shoulder to cheek.

Royal shifts his aqua blue eyes from Clarity's face to mine, taking our measure. "If you pull this off, you'll be on the radar of every intelligence group in the world. They may not know who you are, but the fact that you exist will be out there. If there is someone after the drive, it will put a target on your backs."

I turn to my teammates. Lotus meets my eyes, giving a slight nod.

Clarity touches her hand to my shoulder.

Vale stands, hands in pockets, studying the floor at his feet. Then he looks up at me, conveying everything I need to know with his eyes. He's in this with us, no matter what happens.

I wish I could grab his hand, but I turn back to Royal. "We're ready. We'll finish this."

Royal nods. "Then let's go over our plan one more time. The freighter is set to arrive in three days and we have to be ready."

Royal's questions are brutal. He attacks even the smallest details of our plan, but we're ready for him. We've done it before—dissecting our tactics and turning them inside out in a search for possible complications—so we're ready for most of the scenarios he throws our way.

Finally, he sighs, a proud gleam in his eye as he looks at each of us. "You're ready." He looks down at his watch. "We'll meet for dinner in three hours. Sound good?"

My teammates nod.

"Lotus, you can pick the place, since you're almost a pilot now." He winks at Lotus, who grins.

"All right! I've got some ideas. I'll let you know." He trots out of the room, already focused on a restaurant app on his watch.

Vale glances at me before following him.

"I'd like to visit a couple of local temples, and maybe the Batu Caves," Clarity says. "You coming, Sis?" She grabs my hand.

I put light pressure on her fingers before dropping her hand. "I'll catch up to you."

She smiles. "Bye, Dad." Then she follows the boys down the hall.

I watch them go, the wheels in my head churning out thoughts. Something has been bothering me since Darnay sent us to Kuala Lumpur to retrieve the drive. "Sir?"

Royal looks up at me from where he has settled at the desk, his laptop open in front of him. "What is it?"

I step toward him. "Why didn't Mr. Darnay come to Malaysia himself to retrieve the drive? He's ex-British intelligence, right?"

Royal studies me for a moment, and sighs. "He quit doing field-work almost twenty years ago, after his wife was killed."

My mouth drops open. Darnay lost his wife, like we lost my mom. I mean, I don't know how she died, but I bet the soul-crushing sense of loss was the same. And, like Darnay, it caused my dad to quit going on missions. Instead, he chose to stay closer to home, with me. The only trip he made for a long time after that was his visit to Sicily, when he brought Clarity home. "What about his son? Why don't they live together?"

Royal rubs his smooth-shaven cheek before responding. "I don't know. Charles keeps him well out of the press." His eyes falter, falling to gaze at his clasped hands. "I simply don't know. When Charles and I were in the field, they strongly discouraged us from divulging any personal information to anyone, even our closest friends." He returns his gaze to me. "I don't even know how his wife died."

I chew the inside of my lip. This information, and seeing Royal like this, is jarring. His regret presses him down like a weight on his back. "I know so little about my best friend in the world." The man who shows up in almost all of the stories that aren't too classified for Royal to tell us. "So why do you teach us, our team, not to share personal information if you regret not being there for Mr. Darnay?"

He cuts his eyes at me. "I regret it, but I still think it's wise. You can't trust anyone in this game, at least not forever. Even the closest allies can be turned, given the right application of leverage."

My eyebrows raise. I avert my eyes from him, willing my face to remain blank. He can't know how much Vale and I have told each other about our families and ourselves. I have told Vale everything, except the one intangible gift I have left from my mom: my real name. I turn to face Royal, working to get the words out. "That's a pretty cynical view, don't you think?" I shift on my feet.

Royal stands, moving around the desk toward me. Gently, he reaches out and puts a hand on my shoulder, locking eyes with me. "Loveday."

We're peering at each other, weighing our mettle. Neither of us flinches. I lick my lips. "Yes?"

"I have lost a lot of co-workers, and friends, over the years. And the one thing I've learned is that you can't truly trust anyone. Do you understand?"

I reach up and put my hand over his. "I do."

He puts light pressure on my shoulder, forcing me to hold his gaze. "Promise me you'll keep any private information to yourself, that you won't tell anyone about your background, not even Vale or Lotus."

My eyebrows shoot up. "Not even them? Dad!"

"Not even them."

I push his hand away as if it was a red-hot poker burning into my flesh. "If I can't trust them, then why are they on our team? Why do they live in the Ivory Tower?"

"You don't understand." Royal's voice is grittier now. Frustration seeps through. "I do trust them, or I would never have brought them in, but that may not always be the case. Even if someone is loyal, what if they're captured? Most people talk, given enough time. If they know anything and they're coerced into talking, enemies could find you and Clarity. And I can't lose my girls."

I roll my lower lip inward and bite down on it. "If they were compromised, wouldn't Lotus or Vale lead the bad guys right to the Tower?"

Royal's entire frame tenses. "I have security measures in place for that eventuality." He stares at me for a moment more. "Do we understand one another?"

I nod. "Yes."

The seconds tick by, and my heart is racing.

Finally, Royal steps back, toward the desk. "Then we won't speak of it again."

I swallow as I turn to leave. I know what I have to do, and it's going to nearly kill me to do it. But if what Royal just said is true, and I know without a shadow of a doubt that it is, I have to do it. I have to end things with Vale, before anyone gets hurt.

Chapter 27

Haru is cleaning the bathroom when Clarity and I burst into our hotel room after our exploration of the Batu Caves. Outside the cavern, there was a giant, golden statue of the Hindu god Kartikeya that glittered in the sun. And the stairs! Wow there were a lot of stairs. The caves themselves were awesome, but my favorite part was the monkeys. They're like tiny, furry thieves who run amok over the area around the caves, stealing water bottles, snacks, and anything else they can get their grubby hands on. One even jumped on Clarity and wrapped itself around her neck in an attempt to snag her granola bar. I'm still laughing about it.

Haru stops when she sees us, a cleaning cloth in one hand and a spray bottle of smelly chemical cleaning solution in the other. "I'm almost done," she says, barely above a whisper.

I stifle my laughter. "No problem. We'll wait in the hall." I gesture for Clarity to follow me out.

"Thanks for all the work you do," Clarity tells Haru, patting the bathroom door frame and following me out into the brightly lit hallway. We walk the length of it and look out the floor-to-ceiling window that overlooks the park. Motorcycles and cars zip up and down the road that runs the length of the green, tree-lined space. People mill about, walking, jogging, or lazing on benches and picnic blankets.

"I'm going to miss it here," Clarity says after several minutes. "I didn't realize how hard it is living underground until we got here."

I nod. I've been feeling the same way. The sun and greenery around us here in Malaysia have brightened us all, lifting our spirits and filling our bodies with bounce and vigor. "We've got to do a better job of getting outside once we're home, not just when we're working."

"Agreed."

Footsteps approach behind us. Clarity and I both spin around, our hands going to the weapons we have concealed on our persons.

It's Haru, walking up the hall toward us, pulling the housekeeping cart behind her with one arm, her eyes darting back and forth. "I don't have long before my mom gets back," she says, "but I wanted to ask you a question." She's less timid now, more eager. But what could she possibly want to ask us? Wariness at her approach wars with curiosity at what she could want. Curiosity wins.

"Shoot," I say.

A frown flickers over Clarity's face, but she quickly replaces it with a placid smile.

"Lotus has told me that you attend a private boarding school?" The girl lifts her chin, meeting our eyes. She has to look pretty far up to look Clarity in the face. My sister has a good six inches on me, and even more over Haru.

Clarity looks to me, waiting to follow my lead.

"That's right," I say. "We're here on a school trip, to visit the different temples and mosques here in the city."

"We saw the Batu Cave and the Sri Mahamariamman

Temple today. They're both beautiful," Clarity adds.

Haru gives a faint smile. She isn't interested in our itinerary. "How do you apply to this school?"

Clarity and I exchange a look. "It's very selective," I say, "and hard to get into." I bob my head to emphasize my words.

"Please," Haru says. "I want to study technology, and Lotus has told me that's what you all study at your school."

I keep my face blank, but inwardly I'm cringing. What else has Lotus told her about us? Maybe Royal was right to advise us to be wary.

Haru bites her lip but doesn't look away.

I sigh. "I'll mention you to Royal, okay? I can't promise anything." I can promise nothing. There's no way he'll bring this girl back to the states with us. There's no point in getting her hopes up. Lotus should have known better.

"Thank you, thank you," Haru says, beaming. "I will be truly grateful."

"My pleasure," I say.

Haru clasps her hands excitedly. "You have no idea how excited I am at the prospect of leaving housekeeping work behind."

"Haru!" Her mom yells from down the hall, then continues in firm Japanese.

Haru shrinks at this, glancing over her shoulder. "I have to go. Thanks!" Her eyes shine as she turns and pushes the cart up the hall away from us as quickly as she can.

Clarity and I turn to each other. "What are you going to tell Dad?"

"Everything, of course."

"Oh, Lotus is in trouble."

"You think?" I say sarcastically, then march down the hall.

"I already know," Royal says when I'm done telling him about the conversation Clarity and I had with Haru. He looks down at me, arms crossed, from where he's leaning against the wall of his hotel suite.

"What? Are you serious?" My voice rises as I speak at the thought of our team, our lives, being jeopardized by Lotus's loose lips. "What are you going to do about Lotus?" Anger and disappointment war within me at my teammate's actions.

Royal frowns. "Loveday, control yourself."

I glare at him, choosing to ignore his command. "No. This isn't the time for *restraint*."

He straightens and moves toward me, his face softening.

I stand upright and rigid. I am right about this; it's worth being angry about.

Royal stops right in front of me, and then he does something he hasn't done in a very long time. He wraps his arms around me and pulls me into his chest. "It's going to be fine. You have to trust me in this."

At first I remain tense, but the feel of his comforting arms around me makes me relent. "It's so hard." I whisper.

"I know, but Haru is smart. I looked into her test scores."

I pull back enough to look him in the face. "So? I'm smart."

He chuckles. "Yes you are. So is she. I noticed her mom putting her down, so I did a little research. I asked Lotus to talk to her."

I push him away. "You did? Without asking me?" My mouth clamps shut as soon as the words are out. I've gone too far, but my anger is still simmering beneath my skin, so I make no move to take them back.

Royal's expression hardens. He slides his hands into the pockets of his slacks. "I give you a lot of leeway, but this is my team. Don't forget that."

His words sour in my chest. He's wrong. This is my team. I'm the one who goes through every training with them. I'm the one right beside them throughout every trip into the field. Day in and day out, they are my teammates, my team. But I don't dare argue with Royal. "Yes, sir." I push the words out through clenched teeth.

"Good."

I spin on my heel and get out of there as fast as I can, mumbling to myself about Royal and Lotus all the way up to the roof of the hotel.

It's midday, and a warm breeze wafts over me as I step out onto the roof. The whole space is dotted with lounge chairs. Oversized, squishy cushions lend splashes of color, and large pots spilling over with plants provide much needed greenery.

I weave through the groups of chairs and stand at the edge of the roof, looking down. There's a high wall of plexiglass circumventing the space, probably to make jumping more difficult.

The people on the street below bustle about, living each moment unaware that spies live and work among them, and it has to stay that way.

I reach down and tap a message into my watch.

Me
Meet me on the roof.

The response comes almost immediately.

I stand in the quiet, working to calm my mind. The team is Royal's too, and he wouldn't bring anyone back to the states, to the Ivory Tower, with us unless he trusted him or her. He must have done a lot more research on Haru than he let on. That's for sure.

The door to the roof creaks open. I whirl to face it.

A man in relaxed-fit jeans, a gray sweatshirt, steel toed boots and heavy work gloves steps onto the roof. His hard hat is low over his face, obscuring my view. The nerves in my brain tingle; there's something familiar about him. It hits me—it's the way she walks when she's dressed as a man.

"Clarity."

She lifts her face. "How'd you know?" Her height is massive as she clomps over to me, the scuffed brown work boots on her feet making my sister even taller than normal.

"Your man walk." I turn back to the glass wall. A light breeze rustles the leaves of the tall trees in the park below.

"Shoot," Clarity says, propping an elbow on my shoulder. "I'll have to work on that." Her gaze drifts down toward my face. "Why did you want to meet?"

Despite my rationalization of Royal's actions, the anger that built during my conversation with Royal still simmers on the front burner of my mind. All I need to do to get it boiling is turn up the heat. Instead, I stare down at the sidewalk below. "Did you know Royal *asked* Lotus to talk to Haru about our 'school?'"

Her eyes go wide, but then a smile rises to her wide mouth. A giggle escapes her.

"What's so funny?" I ask, annoyed.

Clarity raises an eyebrow at me. "Think about it."

I purse my lips. "He's feeling the itch to take in another stray?" The words bite as soon as they're out of my mouth. I wish I could gather them up and shove them back down my throat.

My sister's face falls, her mouth hardening. "What a vile thing to say."

Guilt twists my insides. No matter how mad I am at Royal, it's not my sister's fault. "You're right. I'm sorry. I shouldn't have said that."

Clarity's face softens; she's about to cry. "Is that what you really think of Lotus? Of me?"

"No." I wrap my arms around her waist and bury my face in her sweatshirt.

The tension in her frame trickles down to the floor and away, sweeping down toward the ground from our perch high in the air. She puts her arms around my shoulders and rubs my back. "I know what's going on," she says into the top of my head.

I pull back and meet her eyes, my face warm and tingling. "What?"

"You're mad that he made a decision like this without talking to you first."

I remain still, allowing my silence, my lack of a denial, to confirm her statement.

She nods. "I thought so." She pauses, looking down over the city. "Next time, take it out on a cardboard cutout at the shooting range, okay?"

I nod, lifting my eyes toward a helicopter that's zooming overhead. "Deal."

"You haven't said anything about my disguise," Clarity says, splaying her arms to give me a full view.

"Your mustache is too thick. Reel it in a little, and you'll be set."

Clarity grins. "I can do that. You think I'll pass for a longshoreman?"

"Definitely. The baggy clothes hide your figure. The only reason I had you pegged was I know your walk. No one else will be able to tell."

"It helps that I'm tall, for a girl." She ruffles my hair, laughing.

I swat away her hand, my face cracking into a smile.

"There she is," Clarity beams, jabbing me in the side with a finger.

I recoil to avoid further tickling, grabbing her fingers in mine. "Stop it." Our laughter floats away on the air.

"I'll hold her for you," says a low, male voice, just before two hands shoot out and snake around my waist, pinning my arms against my sides.

Instinct kicks in. I lift my foot, slamming it down on my attacker, using the loosening of his grip to shove my elbow into his side. His hands drop and he hunches over, trying to catch his breath while holding his arms tight around his chest. Vale. His face is red as he puffs out a heavy breath. "Ouch," he wheezes.

"Serves you right," I say, also trying to slow my breath. "Never grab me from behind like that."

"Never again," Vale says, his breathing still labored.

"It looks like you need some practice taking someone from behind," Clarity says, eyeing us with a faint smile on her lips.

"I'm all ears," Vale says, pushing himself upright. "Is this your outfit for the shipyard?"

Clarity nods. "I have clothes for you and Lotus too."

In spite of his ragged breathing, Vale smiles. "Excellent. I'm so ready for this."

My heart twists. Once he's on the job, every single person I care about will be choosing to put themselves in danger. If love isn't trusting them to come back alive, I don't know what is.

Chapter 28

The freighter is set to arrive at Port Klang in two days, which means there isn't a lot of time left to prep. Almost everything is set, including our plan once the freighter docks. Clarity has all necessary disguises ready, Vale has hacked into the shipping company's system and created identities for the team so that once we arrive at the dock we'll be treated as longshoremen and let through security without any problems. Lotus is scoping out all of the possible routes to and from the port and testing the traffic flows at various times of day so he'll know which escape route to take once we have the thumb drive. That's where he is now—sitting in traffic on his way back from the port.

Royal and Julep are down at the port, staking out the shipyard in case the cargo ship arrives early.

All that's left to do is prep Vale.

"So, what are we up to today?" he asks from across the restaurant booth, sending me a wolfish grin.

"Down, boy," Clarity says, shooting a look at me.

I push back my plate and all that remains of my breakfast. "Close quarters combat." I slide out of the booth and wait for Clarity and Vale to do the same. "There's a gym down the street with a mat we can use."

Clarity's face opens into a toothy smile. "Excellent."

Vale stands and hovers over us. "I'm ready."

"You'd better be." I lead them out of the restaurant toward the hotel lobby. It's pretty crowded with guests checking out, dragging large rolling suitcases behind them toward the service counter. Movement to the side of the room catches my eye. Haru is watching us from the hallway to the kitchen. The moment my eyes hit her face, she ducks out of sight. I file it away for later investigation and turn back to my teammates. "Get changed and meet back here in five."

"Get off the floor," I yell at Vale, who is struggling to rise to his feet while Clarity fights to keep him off balance. "The longer you're on the floor, the more likely you'll get stomped on or bashed in the head." I sound gruff, I know, but I can't help it. He's got to understand how serious close quarters combat is, and why we avoid it whenever possible. It's why we mostly use tranquilizer guns when we're working. They're effective, and they prevent harm—to us or the people we're working around.

Vale manages to break Clarity's hold on him and clamber to his feet. Before she can regain her balance, Vale does a perfectly timed leg sweep, and Clarity's back down again. He feigns a knee stomp, then stands back. He's won.

"Nicely done," I say, clapping.

"Thank you," Vale says as he leans down to offer Clarity a hand, which she takes.

"Good job today," she says once she's on her feet. "You're getting so much better."

"Thanks!" Vale is beaming under his sweaty brow. He wipes his face with a hand towel, then takes a swig of his water.

Clarity moves over to me, fanning herself with her hand. "He's doing well."

"He is." As much as I hate to say it, Vale is, for all intents and purposes, field ready.

"Let's go again," I say, walking toward Vale. "But this time, you'll be fighting me." My fighting style is different from Clarity's, which will be good practice for him.

Vale's wide eyes shoot up to my face. He licks his lips, hesitant.

"You can't be afraid to fight a pretty girl," I say, walking to the center of the mat.

"Hey!" Clarity interjects from where she sits at its edge.

I wave her off, my eyes not leaving Vale. In a slow, deliberate move, I turn away from him, presenting my back. "Let's work on attacking from behind." My heart rate increases, my body ready for what's coming. My mind wanders back to the first time I did this: Royal had a friend of his come and teach Clarity and I our first self-defense moves. The guy spent a week with us before giving us our final test. He dressed in a giant padded suit and attacked us, one by one, from every angle, making sure we could get free of any hold, land a solid hit or kick, and get out of there. It had been exhilarating and terrifying. I had felt like a superhero by the end of it, when our instructor was leaning over, wheezing from being kicked to the ground again.

My eyes rove around the studio as I wait for Vale's attack. At the other end of the long room, a taekwondo class is just ending, and lots of pairs of eyes are turned toward us. They're standing in a row of white uniforms, not moving.

Vale's arms snake around me in a bear hug, and I get to work, lowering my center of gravity. Once I'm able to wiggle my arms, I put my elbows in play, jabbing at Vale's ribcage. His grip loosens, and I take advantage. A well-placed foot stomp frees me, and a side kick puts him down on the mat.

A few claps sound from across the room. I ignore them. I'm not here for show.

I stand over him, breathing hard. "What was your mistake?"

He lies there, holding his side and panting. "Grabbing you too high?"

"That's a start. Try again."

We go through it a few more times until both Vale and I have won a few bouts. We're both sore and breathing heavily when Clarity walks to the center of the mat, separating us. "I think that's enough for today," she says, putting a hand on each of our shoulders. "Now that you've kicked the crap out of each other, let's go for a swim." She shoots a smile at us and leads the way out of the gym.

I push off the bottom of the pool and shoot toward the sunlight streaming down from the surface. My head pops out of the water, and cool rivulets run down my face and neck. I wipe my eyes and look around.

Vale is swimming laps along the other edge of the pool, his movements slow and deliberate. I want to watch him as his body glides through the water, but instead I force my eyes away. It would not be a good idea to be caught staring at him, especially since I have to break things off with him as soon as the mission is over. Royal is right: letting emotion get involved in our work is a huge mistake. I'd recuse myself from the mission if I thought he wouldn't kill me once he found out my reason. No, he can't know about Vale and me. Ever. And this way, he'll never find out.

I swim toward the edge of the pool and prop myself up on

my elbows. "How's it going?" I holler at Clarity, who is stretched out on one of the lounge chairs on her stomach and reading *The House on Mango Street*.

She looks up at me and smiles. "It's heartbreaking."

I bob my head. "Good. That's good, right?"

Clarity nods slowly. "It's perfect."

Water ripples around me and Vale glides up to me, pulling himself up onto the pool deck. "I'm thirsty. Want anything?"

I look into his green eyes for just a beat too long.

"Loveday?"

My gaze falls to the concrete, which is stamped to look like cobblestone. "No, thanks."

"All right." He snags his towel off a lounge chair and lopes away toward the refreshment stand at the far end of the pool area. I follow him with my gaze, watching the lines of his calves. Ugh. I'm only making it worse.

"Sis." Clarity's voice is tight, alert.

My eyes meet hers. "What?"

She holds up her wrist, drawing attention to her watch. "The ship is here. We have to go." She jumps off her lounge chair, throws her book into her woven bag, and pulls her aqua blue caftan over her head.

Hoisting myself out of the pool, I dig my watch out of my unspooled towel and strap it on. It's waterproof, but I don't like swimming with the clunky band on my wrist.

Then I spy Vale's watch under his lounger, next to his dry T-shirt. Spinning around, I shout. "Vale. We have to go."

He must sense the urgency in my voice, because he sets the umbrella drink the bartender just gave him down on the counter and jogs toward me. "What's going on?" he asks when he's within speaking range.

"The ship is here," I say. "It's time."

I work to keep my heartbeat slow and steady as we rush upstairs to our rooms. I throw on my black jeggings, loose tee, knit cap, and tennis shoes. My heavy duty gloves are shoved into my back pocket. My holster is weighed down by my handgun. It's heavier than my tranquilizer gun, but Royal insisted we use "real" guns since we don't know exactly who was behind the theft of Darnay's car, and possibly the thumb drive.

I stand in the hallway with my back against the wall, spinning the car keys around my finger, while Clarity, in her male dock worker disguise, lumbers down the hall to Vale's room. He responds after one knock, looking remarkably similar to Clarity in dress, though not as tan.

Once they've drawn parallel to me, I catch Vale's eye. "You ready?" I whisper. "There's no going back now."

Vale stops, and, lifting my chin with his fingers, kisses me lightly. "I'm ready. I can do this," he breathes as he pulls away. It's worded like a statement, but there's a question in his eyes.

I take his hand and give it a quick squeeze. "I wouldn't let you step out of this building if you weren't ready."

This steadies him. He smiles at me. "Okay, let's go."

We make our way out to the unmarked white van Royal rented after Darnay told him what was really on the thumb drive. He said it was because it provides more cover than our motorcycles in case of a shootout, which was a little over-cautious, but true, so I didn't argue. So far, Royal's vigilance has kept him alive and in one piece. We hop in, Vale in the back, Clarity in the passenger seat, and me driving, and head toward Port Klang.

I connect my watch to the van's stereo system via bluetooth and put on my Marvel movie soundtrack playlist. A song from *Captain America* comes on and I relax into my seat.

"Do you think it was a coincidence that Mr. Darnay's car was stolen with the thumb drive inside?" Clarity asks, turning to look at me.

I've thought through this again and again since Lotus told us the news a few days ago, but even so the question catches me off guard. I listen to the music for a few seconds, trying to decide how to answer. As team leader, it's my job to give my teammates just enough information to do their jobs, and not enough to freak them out. "There haven't been any signs that it was more than a random car theft." Except that the thief was good enough to sneak past Lotus in the parking lot. And they loaded the car on the freighter and left port only a few hours after the car was secured in the shipping container. It's an awfully big coincidence if Darnay's car, the one with the thumb drive, just happened to be the last one they stole. Royal says there is no such thing as coincidences, not in intelligence.

As we drive, skyscrapers and corporate buildings give way to houses and apartment buildings, and then to empty lots dotted with older, rural properties. The sun begins to set, falling toward the horizon, turning the sky red.

I tug on the back of my knit cap to pull it down over the nape of my neck. "We'll be there in ten. Get ready." I meet Vale's eyes in the rearview mirror. "Expect everything to go wrong, so when it doesn't you'll be pleasantly surprised."

"And if it does?" His eyes glint and his voice is smooth, half joking.

"You won't be caught off guard." I pull into a parking space outside the building where Royal and Julep are stationed on the roof, watching us with state-of-the-art surveillance equipment. The sun is almost below the horizon now, and rays of coral pink and tangerine orange shoot across the sky, their reach lessening as the sun sets beyond the water.

Royal
Lotus is waiting for you at the restaurant. He's saving a table.

Me
Great. I'm starved.

"Everybody out," I say, falling behind as Clarity and Vale saunter along the frontage road that runs parallel to the dock. A dinged-up white car sits at the side of the road. Lotus is sitting in the driver seat, drumming on the steering wheel.

Vale slides into the front seat and fastens his seat belt. Clarity sets a duffle bag on the closed trunk before getting into the back seat on the driver's side. Lotus climbs out of the car and grabs the bag Clarity left him. Using the key fob, he pops the trunk and ducks behind its lid to change into his dockworker disguise.

I turn away from him to give him privacy as he undresses.

Once he's done, he stuffs his extra clothing into the corner of the trunk and climbs back into the driver seat. I scan the area for bystanders and, seeing none, crawl into the trunk and pull it shut.

"Are you ready?" Vale asks through my earbud.

"All set," I respond, curling on my side with my feet tucked. I got trunk duty since I'm the smallest, and because I almost had the thumb drive in London. I want to be the one to finish the job.

The car rolls into motion and I lurch forward, just catching myself before I face plant into the worn gray fibers that make up the lining of the trunk.

A minute later the car slows.

"I'm approaching the security booth," Lotus says into my

earbud. "Here we go."

I hear the low hum of the window being rolled down.

"Afternoon," Lotus says, presumably to the security guard.

"Afternoon," another voice says in response. "Badge please."

I'm still and quiet as I wait, knowing that Lotus is flashing his forged security badge for the guard.

"Go on through."

"Thanks."

The car moves forward, presumably past the security gate, and after a minute, it stops. I'm relying on my team to be my eyes and ears until it's safe for me to climb out of the trunk.

"We're in the parking lot now," Lotus says, for my benefit and Royal's. "The shipyard is directly in front of the car, a few rows up."

I conjure an image in my mind of the high chain link fence, a gate rolled to the side to let vehicles through. "How does it look?"

"It's getting dark fast, but the yard is lit up pretty well," Lotus pauses. "You'll have a hard time finding shadows to slink through."

"Stay to the north side of the yard," Clarity adds. "There's less activity on that side, and there are a few shipping containers they've already emptied. You can hide behind them."

"Proceed," Royal says into our ears. "They're preparing to unload our container."

"Yes, sir," Vale says.

The car doors open and shut, and a knock on the trunk sends a jolt through me.

"Shit, you scared me," I hiss.

Lotus's laughter filters through the earbud. "Sorry," he

chuckles. "Just saying hi." He's not sorry now, but he will be. I'll get him back later, once we're off the job.

"The parking lot is pretty clear," Clarity says, her voice hushed. "Come on out. We're heading into the yard."

I pull the travel flashlight out of my belt and turn it on so I can scan the trunk for the plastic tab that opens the hatch from the inside. It's broken. My throat constricts, but I'm trained to stay calm in these situations. I go completely still and take three deep breaths, in through the nose and out through the mouth, extending my inhale and exhale each time. "The escape tab is broken," I say once I'm sufficiently calm.

Lotus curses. "I'll come let you out."

"You didn't make sure it was functional?" Royal asks, his voice even, unruffled. "No matter. Loveday, find the long cable connected to the locking mechanism and pull on it. That should do it. Lotus, Clarity, and Vale, report for your shift. You're two minutes late."

My teammates voice their assent, their steps echoing in my ears. I can hear them signing in with the shift manager and being assigned tasks.

I turn my focus back to my own predicament. The beam of the flashlight catches every piece of grit embedded in the trunk lining as I pivot in place, looking for the cable that runs to the lock. Once I find it, I pull. The trunk pops open slightly, and I peer through the slit into the parking lot. "Is it clear?" I whisper.

Clarity grunts. "Hold on, let me set this crate down." I hear scuffling and heaving. "Yes, it's clear."

I open the trunk and slide out into the dark space behind the car. Lotus has smartly parked as far away from the lights as possible. He's in the second to last row away from the stir of movement in the yard. There's only a single row of cars beyond his. I begin to move away when I notice something: the cars in the last row are nicer than most of the other cars in the lot. Bingo. These are the stolen cars. I count fifteen total, a mix of vehicles from all of the top luxury brands.

"Did you see the line of luxury cars in the lot?" I ask. "They're stolen. They all have British plates."

"Yes," Vale says. "We walked right past them."

"Did anyone bring GPS trackers?" I ask. "We can tag them on our way out of the lot, once we have the thumb drive, and hand the tracking over to the local authorities."

"I have a bunch in the car," Lotus says. "It's probably enough."

"Do it after you have secured the drive," Royal says.

"Will do." I skirt between the cars, keeping low as I advance toward the yard where the dock workers are bustling around, loading and unloading boxes from forklifts. There are two cranes near the south end of the yard, and they're being used to unload shipping containers from the freighter.

"Our container is next," Royal says into my ear.

I duck behind a shipping container near the north edge of the yard and scramble on top of it. I'm pretty sure it's already been unloaded, because there isn't anyone within twenty yards of it. I flatten myself against the corrugated metal and wait, watching the men on the freighter secure our shipping container for unloading. A light breeze caresses the back of my neck.

The screech of a heavy door opening makes me press my cheek flat against the metal. The voices of two men reach me. They're standing outside the container next to mine. "Move these to the south edge of the parking lot."

I relay the information to my teammates. "Maybe I should go back to the lot, wait for the car there, and get the thumb drive once the men have returned to the yard."

The men enter the container and work inside for several minutes. Then a car starts. Someone drives it slowly out of the container toward the parking lot.

"Hold," Royal says. I can tell by his voice that he's concentrating on something else. The line is quiet for several seconds. "There are several cars coming through security now, and they're heading your way. Keep alert."

I twist and peer toward the parking lot. Royal is right; there are three large SUVs coming into the lot. They don't bother to use designated spaces. Instead, they pull into a semi-circle to one side of the stolen cars, and several men climb out of each of the vehicles. One by one they get into the stolen cars, start them, and leave the lot.

"It's no good," I say. "They've already started taking the stolen cars. I'll have to get the drive before they move Darnay's car to the lot."

"Now's your chance," Lotus says.

I look up. Our container is being lowered into the shipyard. It settles with a dull crunch against the pavement. I pull my knit cap down, making sure my hair is covered. The area below the container I'm perched on is free of workers, so I jump to the ground, landing as quietly as I can. A quick turn gets me around the side of the container.

There are several men standing in front of our container, waiting for the chains to be unhooked. Once that's done and the crane has begun to move back toward the ship, the men get to work. One steps forward and unlocks the doors swinging them open. They go inside, and, using a system of straps and pulleys, they lower the car in the front of the container. One of the workers slides inside and drives the car out of the yard.

Darnay's car is next.

"I'm not going to have time. We need to distract the workers."

"On it," Royal says. A shot rings through my earbud, and I instinctually recoil.

A second later there are yells across the yard. "Clear the area." The dock workers rush toward the parking lot, away from the center of the yard. I look up, and I can see why. One of the chains holding a shipping container suspended from a crane has snapped, and the container is dangling from the remaining supports. The men have cleared the yard so no one gets pancaked if the container falls.

"Nice shot," I say.

Royal humphs. He's pretty tight-lipped about his sniping abilities, but I'm pretty impressed.

I weave between the abandoned boxes and machinery that litter the yard, moving toward the target.

The wind is picking up, and the ominous creak of the overhead shipping container straining the chains makes me hustle. I don't want to be flattened either.

Hustling across the pavement, I reach the container and slip inside, thankful that its mouth doesn't face the parking lot.

The sound of the crane lowering the dangling shipping container reaches my ears. As soon as it's safely aground, the yard will be awash with workers. I have a minute, maybe less. I clamber onto Darnay's car and slide in through the hole I had cut in the moonroof. Crouching in the passenger seat, I use my utility knife to pry up the gear shift cover. The thumb drive falls onto the floor of the car. I bend down, swiping it up with my steady hands, and I'm out of the moonroof in a flash. "Is it still clear?" I ask as I hover inside the shipping container. I slip the thumb drive into a compartment of my belt and zip it closed. It's not going anywhere.

From outside, I hear the dull scrape of the shipping container hitting the ground.

"All clear," comes the yell I assume is from the yard foreman.

"Get out of there," Vale says into my ear. "You've got a few seconds before they're on you."

I slip out of the container and move around behind it, away from the parking lot. "I have the drive and am heading to the north fence."

"Yes," Lotus says over the comm, a smile in his voice.

"Good work," Royal says. "Stay out of sight."

"Yes, sir." I thread my way through the already emptied shipping containers until I reach the fence, and then move along it toward the parking lot.

Already most of the luxury cars have been moved from the lot. It's a good thing I have the thumb drive. Still, I'm relieved that this appears to be a well-oiled car theft ring rather than a covert bid to obtain classified information from MI6.

"We're on our way to the parking lot," Clarity says over the comms. "We'll be there in two minutes."

"They're moving Darnay's car," Vale says. "We're close behind."

Car headlights shine toward me. I sprint through the dark and duck behind the first car I reach, sliding underneath it.

Lotus's car is several rows over. I'll have to wait until the person driving Darnay's car heads back to the lot before I make a move.

The driver pulls the car to the end of the line of the remaining luxury cars and gets out, leaving the door open. He sets the keys on the roof of the car and ambles back toward the yard.

One of the drivers of the SUVs gets out and walks toward

Darnay's car. He bends to look inside, then shouts after the dock worker. "Hey. Get your ass back here."

The dock worker turns, sees that he's being yelled at, and jogs over, holding his hat in place against the now blustering wind. "Yeah?"

"What happened to the moon roof? And the gear cover?"

The worker shrugs. "I don't know. It was like that when I got in it. They must have shipped it over that way."

The SUV driver shakes his head, his jaw set. "I have specific instructions to deliver these cars in pristine condition, and it wasn't like this when it was loaded into the container." He narrows his eyes at the dock worker, who begins to squirm.

"I swear, it was already like that. Ask anyone."

The SUV driver glares at him and stomps off into the yard. He comes back a minute later, grumbling to himself. Stalking back to his car, the man plants his feet and pulls out his phone. After waiting for the person on the other end to pick up, he speaks. "We've got a problem. It's not there."

My heart drops. "Guys, they know." My voice is so quiet, to avoid detection, that I'm afraid my teammates won't be able to hear me.

A sharp intake of breath is all the response I get. It's Clarity.

"Get out of there, now," Royal says, "As fast as you can."

"Yes, sir." I scan the parking lot. It's a straight shot from my position to Lotus's car. I run toward it, ducking into the still partially-open trunk and pulling it shut behind me with a soft click.

Seconds later, the car's doors open and shut, the weight of my teammates making the vehicle sink lower to the ground.

"Everybody in?" I ask.

"Yes," Lotus says. "Should I start the car?"

He doesn't have a choice. The thieves know the drive is missing, and we have to get out before they start searching everyone. Lotus will have to drive right by the three SUVs to leave the parking lot.

I take a deep breath. "Whenever it looks clear to you, start the car and drive out of the lot, nice and slow. Don't fidget or anything." I lick my lips. "Turn some music on, but keep it low so I can hear," I add. "And have your weapons ready."

I unclip my handgun from its holster at my waist and hold it ready. "Ready when you are."

The car starts, and low music filters into the trunk from the cab.

"Here we go," Lotus says.

The car begins to move.

"They're watching us," Clarity says, her voice low.

"Don't make any moves. Just let Lotus steer the car out of the lot. Easy peasy."

"They look suspicious," Vale mumbles. "They're staring at us."

"Stay calm," Royal says.

I'm kicking myself for being in the trunk. Why did I plan it this way? I can't see anything. I can't assess the danger or tell my teammates what to do, how to get out safely. This was a huge mistake.

"They're getting out of their SUVs," Lotus says. "Should I stop?"

"No, don't stop," I say, but I move into a crouch, ready to spring out shooting if I have to.

The car slows.

"Don't stop." My voice is firmer this time.

"We're approaching the security booth," Lotus responds. "So far they aren't following us."

I breathe in. We're going to get out without any problems.

The car goes over a bumpy strip, jostling me.

"We're through," Lotus says, his voice noticeably lighter.

"It looks like we're in the clear," Vale says, sighing.

"Wait." Clarity this time.

That one word makes my mind race. "What?"

"One of the SUV drivers is getting back in the car." She pauses. "He's following us." Her voice is tight.

Lotus curses under his breath, and the car speeds up a tad.

"Royal?" I ask.

"Get out of there," Royal says. "Fast."

"Will do," Lotus chimes.

This time the car lunges forward. I try to hold the crouch, but my legs are burning. I need to do more wall sits once we're out of this.

"They're chasing us." There's a tremor in my sister's voice, which I understand. We've been in car chases before, but usually we're the ones doing the chasing.

"Don't let them catch up," I say. "We don't want a firefight."

The car speeds up, and that's when all hell breaks loose.

Chapter 29

The sound of bullets careening toward us hits my ears.

"They're aiming for our tires!" Lotus yells.

"Loveday, get down!" To his credit, Vale's voice is controlled, albeit higher than normal.

I flatten myself against the trunk of the car, my heart pounding. "Vale, Clarity, return fire."

There's some scuffling inside the cab of the car, and the sound of the windows being rolled down. Two shots are fired. It's my sister. I'd know the sound of her measured shooting anywhere.

A frenzy of shots spirals toward us, and our car jerks to one side. A low, thump hits my ears. Is that...?

"They hit a tire," Lotus yells. "I can't keep this up." The car slows.

The flub flub flub sound of the flattened rubber hitting the pavement makes my stomach churn.

"We're almost to the highway. If we can get there we can disappear in the trees that run along it," Clarity says.

"I don't know if we'll make it that far," Lotus says. The car speeds up again, but the sound the tire is making grows louder, more threatening. It's a good thing Royal had Lotus take a course in offensive and defensive driving with an old friend of his from D.C.'s police force.

More bullets ring out and the car jerks to the other side. "Shit! Another tire."

The car holds its speed, but the sound of the flat tires dragging is sickening.

"Clarity, see if you can disable their SUVs," Royal orders.

"Okay."

"Be careful," I say.

Gunfire rings out all around me. I'm tempted to fire through the trunk's light sockets, but then my protection would be blown.

"Missed! Stupid wind." And then an exclamation. "I got one of their tires!"

"The other SUVs are coming," Vale says, a tremor in his voice.

"Keep it together, everyone," I say, as much to myself as them. A mission has never gone this far sideways before, and I'm not sure what to do.

"Get to the tree line," Royal says. "I'll try to take out the SUVs."

The seconds tick by as I imagine a trio of SUVs bearing down on us, guns blazing.

The crunch of metal on metal sounds behind me, making me jump. And then silence.

But our car is still moving forward, slower.

"What's happening?" I ask. I'd kill for a view right now.

"Royal shot one of the drivers, and he rammed into another SUV. But we've still got one chasing us."

"We're almost to the tree line," Clarity says. "Just another two hundred yards."

"Watch out!" Vale yells.

"No!" Lotus's voice is rough, scared.

A thud jolts our car from behind, sending me rolling toward the far back side of the trunk.

"He rear-ended us!" Vale shouts. "Loveday, are you okay?"

I sit up, rubbing my elbow. Then I roll my shoulders. I'm going to be black and blue tomorrow. "I'm fine."

"Shit," Lotus says. "He's coming again. Brace for it."

I lay down, clutching my handgun, as ready as I can be for the impact. It never comes.

Our car screeches to a stop.

"Guys?"

It's silent.

"Get out of the car!" The voice is loud and close.

"Guys?"

"Another car pulled in front of us," Clarity says. "We're penned in."

My heart is hammering against my chest. Almost my entire family is in that car, and I can't let anything happen to them.

Almost as if Royal is reading my mind, he speaks. "Loveday, wait for the opportune moment."

My mouth opens in disbelief. He's quoting his favorite movie now of all times?! But I listen. "Just say when," I whisper.

"I will," Royal says, his voice steady. "And Loveday, you can do this."

I take a deep breath. I hope to God he's right.

The car door opens and bobbles upward as it is divested of some of the weight it was carrying.

Clarity yelps.

I clench my teeth.

"Where is it?" a man's voice says, loud and commanding.

"Give it to me now, and you can go."

He's lying. There's no way they'll let us go, not if they think we know what's on the drive.

"I know you have it," the man continues.

"What are you talking about? We don't have anything."

It's Lotus, playing it cool.

The sickening sound of flesh on bone rends the air.

"Lotus!" Vale shouts.

"Don't say another word," Royal says into the comms. "I'm taking him out, now." A shot is fired.

I hear a grunt, and then a body hits the ground.

Clarity squeaks. She's just witnessed someone being killed for the first time.

I stifle the urge to punch my way out of this tin can just to be with her, whispering instead. "What's going on?"

There's silence on the line. I hear someone sniff. My sister.

"There are two gunmen left," Royal says. "One of them is using Clarity as a shield. The other has Vale. Lotus is on the pavement, trying to stop the bleeding from a broken nose."

"Okay." I breathe. Scuffling sounds come through my earbud. "Update."

"They're being searched. Can you get to the interior of the car from the trunk?"

Finally, it's my turn to get into the fray. "Hold on." I roll over and get my flashlight out of my belt. Sure enough, there's a lever that lowers the back seat into the cab of the car.

"Yes."

"Do it, as quietly as you can."

I push the lever, but the seat doesn't move. I push harder against it with my shoulder once. Again. My heart beats faster. Why won't this thing budge? I use all the leverage I can get from crouching in the trunk to push my weight against the seat.

Finally it gives way and falls into the cab. I don't move. "Did they hear me?"

"No. They're too busy looking for the drive. But they're smart enough to stay between their hostages and the SUV. I can't get a clean shot."

I close my mind against the image. I can't dwell on it right now. "Is it safe for me to move?"

"Yes."

I crawl through the hole into the back of the car and crouch on the seat, sitting just high enough on my heels to see over the back of the seat toward the SUV. Over my earbud, Royal is whispering to someone else. Julep. I can just hear what he's saying. "Help my kids," he asks her. My heart constricts.

Julep agrees, and through my earbud I can hear feet slapping against the ground. "I'm coming, everyone," she says, her steps quickening to a full sprint. Help is coming in the form of a 5'6" ex-CIA agent, and if I know her as well as I think I do, she's armed to the teeth.

I give myself a mental shake and refocus on the SUV.

The man holding Clarity is doing a fair job of keeping himself behind my sister while he pats her down, so I don't have a good shot at him, the scumbag. On the other side of the vehicle, the guy holding Vale is clearly less experienced. He does a cursory pat down of Vale before repositioning himself behind my teammate's body. Unfortunately for him, he hasn't done a great job. He's left his right side exposed between the side of the SUV and Vale's body. As long as Vale doesn't move, I can get a shot in. It should be enough to free Vale.

I raise my gun and take aim.

"Vale, do you trust me?" I ask, moving my finger over the trigger.

His eyes go wide, but he doesn't flinch.

"Don't move."

He blinks slowly. It's enough.

I take the shot.

The back window of the car bursts, sending thousands of small, pebble-like bits of glass showering over the back seat. The bullet smacks into the hood of the SUV. I pull the trigger again, firing off a second shot.

The man screams, grabbing at his side as he falls backward onto the pavement. He lies there, clutching his lower abdomen.

Vale scrambles away from him toward our car, opening the driver's door to obstruct the bad guys' view before moving to crouch behind the front of the car.

The man holding Clarity isn't moving. He's got his eyes locked on the back of the car where I am hidden. "I know you're in there," he yells.

You think?

"Let her go, and we won't shoot you," I yell back.

"Not a chance," he says. He raises his eyes to the sky.

"Royal?" I ask. But I don't need an answer. The rumble of a helicopter reaches my ears.

Chapter 30

"Incoming," Royal says.

"No kidding," I snap. "How did you miss it?"

"I was lining up another shot, and my spotter is on her way to you."

I shake my head. This is getting chaotic, but once Julep gets here she'll help us regain control of this thing before anyone else gets hurt.

"It's too windy." Royal grunts in frustration. "I'm coming." There is no pause before the sound of his heavy footsteps comes through the comms. Royal, too, is running, though his steps aren't as fast as Julep's. He didn't even pause to pack up his gear. This thought, this truth, is what gets my nerves going. If Royal was careless with his equipment, we're really in it deep.

"Hurry," Lotus says. He stands, wiping the blood from his face, and lifts his gun, pointing it toward the man holding Clarity. "Loveday," he says, his voice flat. He nods toward our left.

I turn my head just enough to look. Shit. Several men from the crashed SUVs are advancing toward us, weapons drawn.

"I'm almost there," Julep says. "I'm in the trees."

I glance over to my right, where the road is banked by a thick stand of trees. She's in there somewhere. There's a flicker of movement and then nothing. My eyes must be playing tricks on me.

The three gunmen advancing toward us from the left slow to a stop about ten yards away. The driver of the SUV is among them. "Hand over the thumb drive," he yells, "and we'll leave."

Clarity's eyes meet mine, wide open and black in her now pale visage; she's terrified.

I aim at the gunmen to my left.

Vale and Lotus keep their sights on the man holding Clarity.

"Hand it over," the SUV driver yells again, "or your friend gets hurt." He nods to the man holding Clarity, who presses his gun against her temple.

Clarity bites her lip, holding herself together, but barely.

The only part of the man holding her that's visible to me is his elbow, and I can't make that shot; it's too risky. Where are Julep and Royal?

"You have five seconds," the SUV driver says, frustration edging his voice. "Five."

I scan the tree line but see nothing. And even if Julep and Royal are there, the man holding Clarity is protected from them by the SUV. They'd have to come out into the open to hit him.

"Four."

My heart is pounding. I never thought I'd have to choose between my sister's safety and the safety of hundreds of allies around the globe.

"Three."

I can't do this. "Wait!" I call. I transfer my gun to one hand and crawl out of the backseat of the car. "I have it." I slip behind the passenger door to give myself some protection in case they start shooting again.

The SUV driver sizes me up, scanning me from head to toe, and grins. "How old are you? Twelve?"

I don't react. People have been underestimating me my whole life, and in my work, it's a definite advantage.

He waits for me to take the bait, and when I don't, he frowns. "Where is the thumb drive?"

Behind us, the drone of the helicopter grows louder. I can feel the wind whipping my back. The helicopter is landing on the street behind us. We're being flanked by enemy combatants.

The SUV driver's attention is diverted to something over my shoulder. He motions with one elbow, and the men at his back pivot, aiming their guns at the trees.

"Don't come any closer," he shouts, then glances at Clarity and her captor. The muzzle of the gun is still pressed against Clarity's skin.

"All we want is the thumb drive," he continues. "Let us have it, and you can go."

"Fine," Royal shouts from the tree line. Quieter, to me. "Loveday, give it to him."

"Roger," I breathe, and lower one hand toward my belt.

The SUV driver's gun is trained on me, watching.

"I'm getting the drive out of my belt," I call, my voice steady despite my shock at what's happening to me and my teammates right now.

He nods, but otherwise remains still.

I unzip the compartment and slide the thumb drive out, holding it up between my fingers. "Let her go and I'll give it to you."

The SUV driver shakes his head. "The drive first."

"It's okay, Loveday," Royal says in my ear.

My heart is pounding. Could I fake a bad throw and catch him off guard? My eyes move to Clarity, who still has the barrel of a handgun pressed to her temple. Damnit. I can't risk it. I take a step toward the SUV driver and mimic tossing him the drive.

The man holds out a hand, and I toss the thumb drive to him. He catches it with ease. "Once we're at the chopper, my man will let your friend go." He and his two compatriots advance toward where I'm standing, guns ready, and then move past us toward the helicopter.

This is when the man holding Clarity makes a crucial mistake. He takes a step forward, pushing Clarity in front of him, exposing his left side to Royal and Julep.

The man flinches back as the bullet enters his side, and he drops his gun.

Clarity lunges forward away from him, scrambling toward us.

Lotus lunges for her, pulling her behind the car with him. There's blood running down Lotus's face from his nose. A wet spot on the front of his black shirt. He puts his arm around her as she trembles against him, fumbling for her handgun with unsteady fingers.

Now I'm angry. These guys are going to pay for hurting my family.

"Now that everyone is safe, let's get the thumb drive back," Royal says. He and Julep run up behind us and take positions on the other side of the car, near the wheel wells.

"Yes, sir," I say. I spin to face the chopper, but the three men are already inside. The heavy metal door slides shut, and the helicopter begins to rise from the ground.

"Vale!" I call. "We have to shoot it down."

"I'm right behind you," he says, his voice calming my fraying control.

I square my stance, take aim, and fire off several rounds toward the helicopter's rudder. The pilot jerks the aircraft to one side, evading my bullets.

Royal comes to stand beside me, gun at the ready. Without looking at me, he speaks. "Lotus and Julep have Clarity. She's fine."

I don't respond. In this, I trust his word. My eyes are locked on the helicopter. It's hovering over us as the man closest to the door slides it open enough to fire at us.

Royal and I duck and press ourselves flat against the side of the car as bullets whizz past. The scent of gunpowder lingers.

A yell bursts from me as I fire as many rounds as I can at the helicopter's rudder, until it looks like someone went after it with a cheese grater. The helicopter begins to spin, then plummets to the ground. A loud crash rings out as the chopper slams into the asphalt, its propeller still spinning.

I don't move. I don't take my eyes off it. The sickeningly sweet scent of blood hits my nostrils.

Three of the men crawl out of wreckage and lay on the pavement, panting and shaking. The pilot wasn't so lucky.

Sirens wail up ahead, and I see the blue flashes of light from the local police force.

Royal is going to have some explaining to do when they arrive; luckily, it's not the first time he's been involved in an incident like this, and he'll know exactly what to say. At least I think he will. Any of his missions that went this far wrong were definitely classified.

Royal rushes forward and takes the thumb drive out of the SUV driver's hand, pocketing it. Then he stands, gun aimed down at them, pinning them in place.

I exhale a deep sigh and lower my gun. It's over.

"Loveday!" Clarity's scream shoots through me like a freezing wind through too thin clothes. My blood turns to ice. I spin around.

She's on the ground crouched over Vale, trying to gather him up from where he is sprawled on the pavement. The shiny red of blood seeps through Vale's fingers as he grabs at his throat.

"No." I fall to the ground beside him, my kneecaps digging into the pavement with a smack. It's like I appeared there. I have no memory of how I crossed those ten yards to where Vale is lying on the ground, his hands at his neck.

There's so much blood oozing between his fingers, between Clarity's fingers.

My stomach twists. I think I'm going to be sick. I clamp the sensation down.

"We have to stop the bleeding," Julep says as she kneels to the ground beside me. Lotus is at her back, standing over us, mouth agape.

Julep reaches toward Clarity's arm and gives a gentle tug. "Let me see."

"No, I can't move my hands," Clarity cries, her voice shaking. "I can't move my hands." Her words are desperate, wild.

"Vale!" I lean over him, trying to catch his gaze, but the light behind his eyes is fading, dark, cloudy. Finally, he manages to focus on me, but his body begins to convulse. He opens his mouth to speak, but it gapes open, no sound coming out.

"Vale," I whisper, taking his face gently in my hands. "Stay with me." Leaning forward, I press a gentle kiss to his sweaty forehead.

He blinks and goes still, eyes wide. His jaw slackens and his hands drop from his neck.

"NO," I scream, my voice high and shrill as my heart implodes into dust in my chest.

Two paramedics scramble toward us, pushing us out of the way. "Give us some room." They kneel beside Vale, working on him, but they didn't see the life leaving his body like I did. I don't have to watch them hang their heads to know that it's already too late.

I make to stand, but topple backward onto my tailbone. Sobs build inside me until I can't contain them anymore. My screaming slices through the air as I again attempt to stand.

One of the paramedics moves to help me, but I kick him away. He jumps out of range, his face lined with sadness. He's seen all of this before.

From where Royal is standing, talking quietly to a police officer, he glances at us—his daughters. His face is grim as he returns his focus to the uniformed man standing before him.

Clarity wraps her arms around me and clings to me, her scarlet hands gripping my shirt, twisting it into a wrinkled, bloody mess, but it doesn't matter. I sink into her shoulder and cry, my eyes squeezed shut.

Chapter 31

I'm silent as Royal debriefs us. Apparently, MI6 has taken custody of the drive, as well as the men who survived the confrontation outside the shipyard. Vale, on the other hand, is lying dead in a casket at the airport, awaiting our arrival.

I can't bring myself to care that we succeeded in reclaiming the thumb drive. I should feel proud that we pulled off our first international mission, but I'm not. Inside, I'm completely numb, cut off from the reality Royal is talking about. My mind keeps returning to the image of Royal standing over Vale's suitcase, packing it up with care. He'll sort through it before he sends Vale's effects to his parents in Greenbow, Alabama.

I never got to meet them, and now I never will. Royal has forbidden us from going to Vale's funeral, forbidden us from introducing ourselves to our fallen teammate's parents. They can't know what we look like, for security reasons.

Once the debrief is over, Royal approaches and sits in the chair across from me. "I'm so sorry," he says, putting a hand on my knee. "Nothing I say will make this easier."

I refuse to look up into his face. The sight of his careworn face will only bring on more tears.

After a minute, he stands. "Meet us downstairs when you're ready," he says to Clarity, who is standing at my shoulder.

She nods, and he leaves, followed by Lotus and Julep.

My sister puts a hand on my back, but I don't move. We remain like that for a long time, not moving or speaking. Finally, I stand. "We should go."

We lug our bags down the hall to the elevator. Royal, Julep, and Lotus are waiting for us in the lobby.

We leave the elevator and walk down the hall to the lobby.

I freeze at the sight of the person standing with the rest of my teammates.

It's Haru, wearing a button-up chambray blouse and pleated skirt, a Sailor Moon backpack slung over her shoulder, a bedazzled phone in her hand.

I narrow my eyes, focusing my glare at Royal. "What's going on?"

Royal rests a hand on Haru's shoulder. "Haru is coming with us to D.C." His face is smooth, empty of emotion, but his stance, shoulders squared with a hand protectively over Haru, says he's not going to argue about it.

I don't say a word. Instead, I pluck my headphones out of my jeans pocket and put them in my ears. I turn on the music app on Vale's phone and turn up the volume. The booming sounds of electric guitars and beating drums fill my ears, drowning out the noise around me.

It doesn't matter anyway. My dad's rules can go straight to hell. I'm not going back to Washington, D.C. At least not right away. I'm going to Greenbow, Alabama.

I may not be able to talk to Vale's parents, but I can observe them for a while, get to know them that way. Besides, it's my fault that Vale is dead, and I won't let them lower him into the ground without getting to say goodbye.

Without getting to say I'm sorry.

After that, I'll head back to Washington, D.C. with one goal: find out who was responsible for the theft of the MI6 files in London, for Vale's death, and bring them to justice. By any means necessary.

Acknowledgements

First, I have to thank you, dear reader, for taking the time to read this book. I am forever grateful to each and every person who reads any of my work. It wouldn't be an author without you, the reader.

Second, no book is the work of just one person. This one came to be with the help of Josiah Davis, a great developmental editor, Christina Kobel, a cracking proofreader, and my husband, my biggest encourager.

Again, thank you. You mean so much to me.

About the Author

Emily lives in sunny Southern California with her husband and daughters. She started writing in elementary school and continued writing in college, where she earned a degree in creative writing. She often gets ideas for stories from the lives of her friends and family. When she's not writing, she enjoys cuddling with her two dachshunds Nestlé and Kiefer, crocheting, watching television, and enjoying the sunshine with her daughters and their flock of backyard chickens.

To learn more about Emily, visit her website: www.emilykazmierski.com

Keep reading for a sneak peek at book two of the Ivory Tower Spies series, *The Eyes of Spies.*

Chapter 1

The wind whips around the skyscraper and slams into my body. I steady my hands as I replace the panel of glass I'd cut through four minutes before. It almost falls through into to the darkened office on the other side, but I catch it just in time. I rush through melding the glass back together with my handheld laser welder since I know the staff at Cobalt Services, from what I've heard, are not to be messed with. Tightening my grip on the rope that suspends me, I begin pull myself upward, but movement inside the building catches my eye. The Cobalt security personnel have arrived.

The men, who are wearing black suits with white shirts and black ties run into the office I have just vacated, their guns drawn and eyes darting around. Despite the generic look of their uniforms, I'm hoping they don't spot me.

But everything doesn't always go my way.

One of them locks his eyes on me and murmurs to the others without taking his eyes off me.

As one unit, the men move toward the window with guns aimed right at my head.

I don't hesitate. In one swipe, I pull my tactical knife out of my utility belt and sever the rope above my head.

My body is plummeting toward the ground.

My watch vibrates, but I don't move to check it. Lotus can wait.

I curl my legs up toward my butt and loosen my arms so they circle my head. I can't say that I've done much urban skydiving, so I'm focused on the asphalt below me, waiting as long as possible before deploying my chute.

3

2

1

The powerful jolt of my parachute opening yanks on my pelvis. It's at once painful and reassuring. Grasping the steering cords on my chute with steady hands, I steer away from the towering glass edifice I've just left. I have to get as far away as I can before their security personnel reach ground level.

I'm low enough now that if I'm within range when they spill out onto the street, they'll shoot at me. And most likely they won't miss.

I glide around the corner, losing altitude the entire way. "Meet me in the alley," I say, knowing my ear bud will pick it up.

"Will do," Lotus says.

My heart is still pounding. That was close. A grin settles on my face. I've done it. The thumb drive is in my utility belt. Once I get back home, Royal, with Haru's help, will be able to dig into Cobalt's recent activities to see if they've been breaking the law like the CIA suspects.

It's only been six months since Haru joined us, since Vale's death… I shake it off. I can't think about that right now. I have to keep my mind clear and ready to take action.

I bend my knees and brace for impact with the concrete, but my feet slam into the ground and my legs crumble, casting me face-first onto the cement. A frustrated groan escapes me as the crisp, white canopy of the parachute billows down around me. After jumping to my feet, I cut the cords. There isn't time to fold the chute properly, so I ball it up and shove it into a trash can on the sidewalk. Pumping my legs, I bolt around the corner of the building into the dark alley.

Behind me, footsteps pound the pavement. Cobalt's security force is catching up.

Crap.

My eyes dart over the long, narrow space. The only hiding place is a large, dingy blue dumpster. Of course. I hurl myself over the side and into the dank black of the giant metal box. The squishy, smelly scent of rotting food folds over me. I move my hips back and forth, slithering down into the garbage. Gooey liquid seeps down my neck into my bodysuit. I breathe through my mouth to avoid the rank smell. Why is it that whenever I need shelter in a situation like this, there's never an industrial sized recycling bin around? Shredded paper would be infinitely preferable to the putrid goop I've found myself in in the past.

"Where are you?" Lotus's voice hums in my ear.

I don't respond as I reach down to unclip my handgun from its holster at my waist. If Lotus is close by he can hear what I'm hearing, and he'll understand.

Heavy boots clump around the corner and halt mere feet from my hiding place.

I breathe silently, slowly, hoping they won't look in the dumpster, but of course they do.

The dumpster eases back toward the wall as a large someone leans over it to peer inside, the metal groaning under the force.

My eyes are wide open, despite the burning starting due to the muck I'm in. I'm staring at the garbage bag above my face, hoping they don't start digging through the trash. It would only take one swipe of the hand for them to spot me, and then I'd be done. I'd be another in the long line of people who have simply disappeared. It takes all of my training to keep calm in this moment, a breath away from oblivion. My hands are wrapped tightly around my weapon, but I'm praying I don't have to pull the trigger. An image of bloody hands flash in my mind's eye.

Come on, Loveday. Focus. I push the image away.

The metal box squeaks as the weight eases off the dumpster and the footsteps move away down the alley.

I take a deep breath in through my nose, but regret it immediately when the stench of eggshells hits my throat.

I stifle the urge to gag, and whisper. "I'll meet you behind the bank in 1 minute."

"I'm already here," comes Lotus's response. "I had to duck out of the alley to avoid the suits. Where are you?"

I ignore it. He'll be able to smell where I was soon enough.

Easing myself into a crouching position, I straighten my legs and peek over the edge of the dumpster. The XCom security force is nowhere in sight. I take a deep breath and hoist myself out of the bin, pushing my legs to their limit. I bolt out of the alley and around the corner to the bank building. It's only 50 yards away.

A shot rings out behind me.

I don't dare look over my shoulder as I round the corner. Lotus is there on his Suzuki, waiting for me.

Taking a running leap, I jump on the back of the motorcycle and snake my arms around Lotus's waist. "Go!"

He guns it.

Several more gunshots reach my ears, but no pain bites into my body.

"That was close," Lotus yells as he maneuvers the bike down the street.

My heart is pounding in my chest, but I know what'll ease the tension. I lean closer to Lotus, digging my pointy chin into the space between his shoulder blades and rubbing in sloppy circles.

Lotus screeches and arches forward away from me without letting go of the handlebars. "Stop that!" he pleads between peals of laughter. "Not while I'm driving!" As if to prove his point, the Suzuki jerks to the right, toward the curb.

"Point taken," I yell in his ear. Without looking back, I retrieve the helmet from the storage box over the back wheel and pull it on over my mousy brown wig.

It's barely 05:00, but the streets are already teaming with commuters. Even so, no one notices us as Lotus weaves expertly between vehicles on the road. People are not nearly as observant as they think they are. They miss pretty much everything.

Chapter 2

Lotus drops me at the hotel's staff entrance and pulls his motorcycle around the corner toward the parking garage exit.

The hall is warmly lit when I step inside. I pass the employee locker rooms, laundry, and supply closets and step into the kitchen. There are only a couple of staffers present, beginning work on breakfast for the buffet. One is muttering to herself as she gathers dry ingredients from the pantry. The other is leaning against the counter nursing a large mug of coffee. Neither one looks particularly alert. My mouth tilts upward. It's a risk I'll take. Neither of them notices me as I duck below the counter and approach the pantry. The woman who was digging around inside seems satisfied with the load of cartons in her arms, because she shuffles around the counter to the other side, near the industrial stove. I peer over the countertop, but coffee girl hasn't seen me either. Snaking one arm above the counter, I swipe a couple kiwis from the bowl and eat them, skin and all. They tickle on the way down, which is why I love them so much. No other fruit does that.

I pivot where I'm squatting near the floor and stare at the fridge thermostat for a minute, itching to try the new entrance Royal has installed to our bunker. The door from the dining room swings open and three more kitchen staffers enter the room. I frown silently, knowing I've missed my chance. Keeping low, I scuttle back through the kitchen and out into the staff tunnel. But instead of moving back toward the parking garage, I continue down the hall toward the lobby. The hotel is a giant cube, with rooms on all four sides facing inward toward the atrium. I crane my neck to look up at the ceiling, a glittering space of glass through which the stars twinkle and blink, shining brightly before fading as dawn breaks.

Since it's so early, the atrium is mostly empty.

There's one hotel patron at the ATM, standing still so the facial recognition software can connect his visage to his account.

I move carefully toward the pond and waterfall that stands in the center of the open space, glowing vivid blue from the lights mounted at the bottom of the pond. One by one, I cross the stepping stones and duck behind the waterfall. A lever, labelled "Waterfall Maintenance," sits against the slimy wall, its rubber coating peeling in places. I pull it downward and a door in the back wall slides open. I step down into the doorway and push a silver button on the wall. The door grinds closed behind me.

When they built this place, Darnay told everyone it was a conference facility, and the brainless baboons bought it. A smirk rises to my lips. Charles Darnay isn't much more than a baboon himself. My mind never can quite wrap around the idea that he was a spy in the glory days when my dad was active. Well, more active. And especially not after the London fiasco.

The steps down to the Ivory Tower are lit by tube lights that flank the stairs. At the bottom, a thick metal door blocks my way. I step to wall on my right and stand with my nose a hair's breadth away from the facial scanner, about 4" square. It beeps three times, letting me know it's scanned and recognized my features, and the metal door slides into the wall, opening the path forward.

Lotus's helmet hangs on a peg on the wall, next to an assortment of jackets, scarves, and accoutrements, but he's not in the den. Lit wall sconces light the room dimly, favoring the two mismatched sofas and handful of plush chairs that sit in what amounts to a circle.

I pull my trench coat off one of the hooks and put it on, buttoning it securely.

Haru bounces toward me, clapping her hands together in rapid motion. "Did you get it? Did you? Did you?" Her entire body hums with kinetic energy, and she swipes at the inside of her right elbow with her left hand. It's an unconscious fidget of hers.

"Yeah." I pull the thumb drive out of my belt and hand it over.

"Yes!" She pumps her fist and shoots away from me toward the control room.

I use my mug to unlock another facial recognition panel and step into the armory. It's a long, narrow room lined with gun safes. We each have one. Well, Haru doesn't. She's only been down in the Tower with us a month and her weaponry skills aren't great, not that she needs them. Royal won't ever put her in the field. But already her computer and coding skills have come in handy.

The safes are lit by cold, white lights that shine upward from the floor. I walk over to my safe and place my right hand flat on the screen set into the middle of the door panel. A small red light in the upper right corner of the screen blinks several times before turning green. I spin the five-pronged handle and pull open the heavy, 6" thick steel door.

A corner of my lip curls up at the sight of my arsenal. I *may* have a few firearms. I stow my Glock and ammo in their proper places, along with my tactical knife. My karambit knives stay on my belt at all times. I close the safe before putting my rappelling gear in the inner room of the armory. It's a small room made of floor-to-ceiling wire mesh cages with everything from binoculars and other surveillance devices to ropes, parachutes, etcetera. I take a deep breath as my eyes rove over the shelves filled with trimmings of my trade. The order of the armory is soothing, especially knowing I could defend myself against pretty much anyone using the tools we keep here.

I pull the bobby pins out of my hair, and whip off the wig. My scalp is itchy under the cap. My bleached, white-blonde hair is slicked back. The roots are dark. Thankfully, Clarity loves extending her cosmetic experimentation to me, and anyone else who will sit still long enough. One time, Clarity accidentally on purpose dyed my hair bright pink with a natural, beet juice dye she wanted to test.

My scalp tingles as I dig my fingers into my hair, mussing my faux hawk so it flops down to the left. The short hair on the sides of my head is pressed flat, but once I'm done rubbing my skin, it's probably sticking out in all directions.

Hoping to avoid Royal, I duck past the control room and into the dormitory. Clarity has added photos of Rihanna to the collage surrounding our door in the few hours I've been gone.

Clarity is there when I shut the door behind me, her long, thick body curled over her vintage, mirrored vanity, makeup strewn across its surface. She turns to me with a broad smile.

I bust up laughing.

Two of her teeth are blacked out and she's sporting a unibrow.

"Who are you today?"

She shrugs. "Just experimenting."

Once I'm clean and changed, I return to my room.

Clarity is still at her desk, inches away from her mirror, putting finishing touches on her eyebrows.

I slide open the bottom right drawer of my desk and kiss a finger before pressing it to my mother's photograph, then to Vale's. The new, shiny black frame doesn't jibe with the older, scratched frame around my mother, but I won't change it. An old loss and a new one, side by side. I run a finger over the bindings of my mom's old, cloth bound books. The gold lettering is fading, and the pages are bent and yellowed, but they're my most prized possessions: the only tangible remnants of my mother. I pick up a small, blue volume, Lucy Maud Montgomery's *Anne of Green Gables*, and tiptoe back across the room to sit at Clarity's feet. She pats my hair absently, says, "We'll bleach this later," and returns her focus to the mirror.

Lotus pops his head in the door. "Royal's called a briefing."

A glance at my watch shows no new notifications. "Why not send a message?"

Lotus shrugs. "I was heading this way anyway."

A sigh escapes as I close my book. I cross the minefield that is our room and set the book back in its drawer where it will be safe.

Clarity stands, stretching her arms and back and making a low groan as she does so. "I've been at that desk for way too long," she says, moving to the door.

"Are you going to take out those black teeth?" I cock my head at her.

"And miss the look on Haru's face? No way." She prances out of the room with what I know is a Cheshire cat smile spread across her lips. She loves to creep out Haru with her experiments.

Order *The Eyes of Spies*, book two of the Ivory Tower Spies series on Amazon.com.

Made in the USA
Middletown, DE
15 July 2019